Book Eight

BY
TONYA KAPPES

TONYA KAPPES
WEEKLY NEWSLETTER

Want a behind-the-scenes journey of me as a writer?
The ups and downs, new deals, book sales, giveaways and more? I share it all!

As a special thank you for joining, you'll get an exclusive copy of my cross-over short story, *A CHARMING BLEND.* Go to Tonyakappes.com and click on subscribe in the upper right corner to join.

ACKNOWLEDGMENTS

Gayle Shanahan! Thank you so much for submitting your Pecan Ball cookie recipe to the annual Kappes Christmas Cookie exchange. I'm so excited to have it featured here at The Bean Hive.

CHAPTER ONE

I liked nothing better than the smell of the freshly made coffees that brewed in the industrial coffee makers. The rich scent of my very own Peruvian roast curled around me like a warm blanket, and Pepper lay at my feet, warming them with his body heat.

Who knew how much a sweet Schnauzer could warm not only my feet but my heart? I reached down and patted him on his sleepy head, but he didn't move. The fireplace glowed with an orange flame and heated the Bean Hive to a perfect temperature for the customers who would arrive when we opened.

The coffee makers beeped to let me know the coffee had been fully brewed, sounding like a wonderful melody. The sound was music to my ears and a signal to get up off the couch and put the breakfast treats in the oven so they'd be hot, fresh, and ready for anyone who needed a little sweet with their morning coffee.

Pepper lifted his head to see what I was doing. "I better get those in the oven," I told him. "It's still coming down pretty good out there."

The entire front of the Bean Hive consisted of windows with a long counter-type bar in front of them. Behind the long bar stood stools for the customers who wanted to enjoy their coffee while taking in the magnificent view of Lake Honey Springs, the actual reason why Honey Springs, Kentucky, was a tourist town. Even in the winter.

"So pretty," I said with a sigh as I looked out at the freshly fallen snow down the pier and across the boardwalk. Then I turned to head back toward the kitchen of my coffee shop.

Bunny Bowowski, my only full-time employee, would be here soon. We took turns opening, and today was my day, which I didn't mind. I'd left my husband, Patrick, and our poodle, Sassy, at home and fast asleep, tucked into the warm bed.

After I went to Pet Palace, our local no-kill shelter version of the SPCA, Pepper had adopted me as his human, and Sassy and Patrick came along later. That reminded me to keep my ears peeled for Louise Carlton, owner of Pet Palace. She said she had a new cat for me to showcase at the Bean Hive this week.

I had gone through a lot of hoops to get the health department to even agree to let me showcase an animal from Pet Palace. Everyone deserved a loving home, and having an animal that needed a home here during the week was a perfect way for people to see how the animal acted and how they might fit together with that animal. I was proud to have been able to help all the animals I'd had in the coffee shop. They were all adopted out and living their best lives.

Louise had already told me a little about the sweet feline, so I was excited to get her into the shop to give her some good loving. It was still a little too early for Louise to show up, but you never knew whether someone was going to be early or not. I certainly didn't want her waiting outside in the snow with the cat.

I dragged the coat rack sitting next to the counter and used the rack to prop open the swinging door connected to the coffee shop and the kitchen just so I could hear if anyone was knocking.

The Bean Hive opened at six a.m. during the week and a little later on the weekends. There wasn't an exact time I opened, but six a.m. was when we got up and moved around. During the winter months I didn't open on Sundays, but I did come in to order and prepare the food for the upcoming week.

We were technically a coffee shop, but I liked to make everyone feel welcome and at home. Coffee was great for that, but a little something for the belly was also good. Each week on the menu I had a breakfast item outside of the usual donuts, scones, and muffins. I provided something like a quiche or breakfast-type casserole with a little more oomph for the hungrier customers. I offered a light lunch as well. These food items were the exact same for a week, so I made them in bulk on Sunday.

The kitchen had a big workstation in the middle where I could mix, stir, add, cut, or do whatever I needed to do to get all the recipes made. Someone might look at it and call it a big kitchen island, but it was where all the magic happened. There was a huge walk-in freezer as well as a big refrigerator. I had several shelving units that held all the dry ingredients and a big pantry that stored many of the bags of coffee beans I'd ordered from all over the world. I liked to roast my own beans and make my own combinations, but the coffee shop had pretty much reached its capacity of what I could roast, and the small roaster was in much need of a bigger upgrade. However, I rented the space from my aunt Maxine Bloom, and there was no room to expand on the board-walk where we were located. On my right was the Queen for the Day spa, and to the left of me was Knick Knacks, a little boutique store with a variety of items. Aunt Maxi didn't own those, so expanding was pretty much out of the question because they weren't going anywhere anytime soon.

Quickly I put the muffin tins in the oven to get them heated up and ready to put in the glass display counter. Then I grabbed the dry ingredients I needed to make the coffee soufflé, which would sell out so fast. Every time I made it, it was a hit. Of course it was amazing. Who didn't like sugar, vanilla, and coffee?

"One envelope unflavored gelatin, sugar, salt and vanilla," I said to myself, plucking the items off the shelf as I found them. "Now for a little brewed coffee." I grabbed the carafe out of the small pot of coffee I kept in the kitchen for me and put it on the workstation with the dry ingredients. Then I went to the refrigerator to grab the milk and eggs.

Eggs didn't really need to be refrigerated, but for some reason I refrigerated them. Everything in the coffee shop was prepared with the freshest of ingredients. If I could get it locally, I did. My honey came from the honey farm across the lake from the boardwalk. The vegetables and eggs came from Hill's Orchard, and the coffee beans came from all over the world.

"Hi do!" From the coffee shop, I heard the familiar greeting from my Aunt Maxi. "It's me! Maxi!" she called out like I didn't recognize her voice.

But I knew she did it to let me know she wasn't some random burglar. Aunt Maxi owned the building where my coffee shop was located, and she had a key. She showed up whenever she wanted.

"Back here!" I hollered back just as I finished pouring the soufflé into a serving dish and putting it into the chiller to set. I had already made some earlier this morning, so I took those out of the chiller and was pleased with how they turned out.

"Oh, coffee soufflé today?" Aunt Maxi walked into the kitchen. She wore a bright-red wool coat with big purple buttons.

"Yes." I couldn't stop from smiling when I saw her.

She also wore a pair of snow boots with her polyester brown pants tucked in. She tugged off the purple knit cap that matched the color of her hair.

"What?" She used the tips of her fingers to lift her already-high hair in place.

"Your hair. I don't think I've ever seen it that purple." I walked over and kissed her.

"Honey, it's a new year. New me." She unbuttoned her coat and hung it up on the coat rack that continued to prop the kitchen door open. Her patchwork hobo bag hung across her body. She dug down deep in it to retrieve a big can of hair spray.

"Seriously?" I asked. "My food," I reminded her, but it didn't stop her from spraying.

"I've got an image to keep up now that I'm in the new play." And that was why she was here.

"Play?" I took the bait to hear all about her new adventure.

Aunt Maxi was always getting into something. I always enjoyed hearing about them even if not all of them had come to be. She was the reason I moved to Honey Springs after my divorce.

Aunt Maxi had always lived here, and when I was a little girl, my father would come to visit, bringing me with him. I loved being here so much I even started to spend my summers here. It wasn't until I'd gone off to college, earned my law degree, gotten married to another lawyer, and opened a law firm with my spouse that I realized our client policy was to help all our clients in more than just law.

Well... that was when I found my now-ex-husband, Kirk, doing counseling than was more than verbal, if you knew what I meant. It was then that I ran off into the arms of my aunt, who just so happened to have this space open while Honey Springs was in desperate need of a coffee shop.

I was still a lawyer and kept my license up. Good thing, too, because I give out so much advice around here that I find it soothes my lawyer side. But coffee was my passion. I loved all things surrounding coffee, and gathering with friends for a little gossip just might be my favorite thing of all. Gossip happened all day long at the Bean Hive. So technically, working here didn't feel like work to me.

"Mmmhhhh. Didn't you notice the new dowel rod flags on the lights around town?" she asked.

Aunt Maxi was referring to the dowel rods on the carriage lights that were all over Honey Springs and the boardwalk. Every season or occasion, the beautification committee had special flags to hang on the rods. It was a special touch to add to our small southern lake town.

"Well, I want you to know that Bunny Bowowski didn't vote for them, and neither did Mae Belle Donovan." She shrugged and curled her nose in disgust. "Low-retta Bebe is the producer of this year's local theater."

Aunt Maxi didn't have to say any more than that. I knew this conversation would need a cup of coffee.

"Grab those muffins and the stack of cookies," I told her. I grabbed the soufflés and the serving tray of mini breakfast quiches I'd made. The pastries were all ready to go in the display case "While we fill the display case, you can tell me all about it."

When both of us were through the door, I put down the items in my hand and moved the coat tree back. Turning back around to look at the inside of the coffee shop, I gasped at the beauty of the coffee shop.

"I'll tell you after I go to the bathroom." Aunt Maxi headed there.

Even though Aunt Maxi owned the building, she didn't give me a cut on the rent. I didn't expect her to since it was part of her income. Rent was a little steep, but I'd watched a few DIY videos on YouTube to figure out how to make the necessary repairs for inspection when I first decided to open the coffee shop. I couldn't've been more pleased with the shiplap wall, which I'd created myself out of plywood and painted white so it would look like real shiplap.

Instead of investing in a fancy menu or even menu boards that attached to the wall, I'd bought four large chalkboards that hung down from the ceiling over the L-shaped glass countertop.

The first chalkboard menu hung over the pie counter and listed the pies and cookies with their prices. The second menu hung over the tortes and quiches. The third menu over the L-shaped curved counter listed the breakfast casseroles and drinks. Above the other counter, the chalkboard listed lunch options, including soups, as well as catering information.

On each side of the counter was a drink stand. One was a coffee bar with six industrial thermoses containing different blends of my specialty coffees as well as one filled with a decaffeinated blend, even though I never clearly understood the concept of that. But Aunt Maxi made sure I understood some people drank only the unleaded stuff. The coffee bar had everything you needed to take a coffee with you, even an honor system that let you pay and go.

The drink bar on the opposite end of the counter was a tea bar. Hot tea, cold tea. There was a nice selection of gourmet teas and loose-leaf teas along with cold teas. I'd even gotten a few antique tea pots from the Wild and Whimsy Antique Shop, which happened to be the first shop on the boardwalk. If a customer came in and wanted a pot of hot tea, I could fix it for them, or they could fix their own to their taste.

A few café tables dotted the inside, as did two long window tables that had stools butted up to them on each side of the front door. It was a perfect spot to sit, enjoy the beautiful Lake Honey Springs, and sip on your favorite beverage. It was actually my favorite spot, and today would be a gorgeous view of the frozen lake with all the fresh snow lying on top.

"Burrrrr. It's cold." Bunny Bowowski walked through the door, flipping the sign to Open. "Me and Floyd enjoyed your soufflé so much last night." She loved talking about her new relationship with Floyd.

Bunny's little brown coat had great big buttons up the front, and her pillbox hat matched it perfectly. The brown pocketbook hung from the crease of her arm and swung back and forth as she made her way back to the coffee bar. There, she'd grab a coffee before she hung up her coat and put on her apron.

"Did you notice the new lamppost flags?" she asked and waddled back over to the coat tree. Slowly she unbuttoned her coat and hung her purse and her coat on the coat tree. The sound of the water running in the bathroom caught her attention. "What was that?"

"Aunt Maxi is here, so maybe you shouldn't talk about the flags," I suggested, since they were probably talking about the same thing and clearly on opposite sides of whatever it was they spoke of. If it was no big deal to either of them, neither would've brought it up.

"Good thing she's here. I'm gonna give her a piece of my mind." Bunny brought the mug up to take a sip.

"Were you flapping your lips about me?" Aunt Maxi stood, glaring at Bunny with her fists on her hips. Her purple hair glistened in the light of the coffee shop.

"What are you doing here so early?" Bunny gave Aunt Maxi the once-over. "You trying to get to Roxy before me, huh?"

"Listen, we are open, and I don't have time for all of this." I looked between the two of them.

7

"Did you not see that snow out there?" Bunny asked. "It took Floyd almost an hour to get me here."

"It takes Floyd an hour to get anywhere without snow," Aunt Maxi muttered under her breath but knew Bunny could hear her.

"Ladies," I said in my warning tone, though I knew it wasn't going to work. "Everyone grab a cup of coffee, and let's talk about what is going on."

Bunny already had her cup and sat down at the café table nearest her. Aunt Maxi sat down at a different table near her. Instead of trying to get them to compromise at a neutral table, I simply let them stay, grabbed Aunt Maxi and myself a cup of coffee each, and stood so I could address them both.

"What are the flags about?" I asked Aunt Maxi, who was busy doctoring up her coffee with creamer and sugar. My eyebrow lifted as I wondered why she even bothered having coffee in the cup.

"They are about the play." She lifted her chin in the air and looked down her nose at Bunny. "Bunny and Mae Belle are mad because they didn't get an offer to be in the play, as I did."

"We don't care one iota about that, Maxine," Bunny chimed in. "We want to use the flags we had last year to promote all of Honey Springs for the winter instead of spending money on new flags when we could use that money somewhere else."

Bunny had a good point, but I didn't dare tell Aunt Maxi. She'd have a conniption right then and there. It wouldn't be a pretty sight.

"What good is doing a play for the tourists if they don't know about it?" Aunt Maxi snapped back. "We could put it in the paper, but tourists don't buy our local paper. We could put it on flyers in the shops, but look at that snow. Who is going to come out in the snow right now?"

Then I could see Aunt Maxi's point.

"Roxanne." When Aunt Maxi said my full name, I knew she truly believed what she was about to say. "I'm telling you, when Bunny thought she had a shot at the lead of Vi Beauregard, she was all over using whatever funds to promote it. Even had the boys at the Moose talking about what a good Vi she'd be."

"Why," Bunny said with a gasp, "I can't help it if the boys at the Moose like me over you, Maxine Bloom. I guess my niceness trumps your gaudiness." Bunny's eyes drew up and down Aunt Maxi until they fixed right up on Aunt Maxi's purple hair.

Aunt Maxi looked like one of those pressure cookers. I could feel her anger curling up from her toes and straight up to her hair. I swear, I thought I saw her hair stand up even more on its own.

"Why, Bunny Bowowski!" Aunt Maxi smacked the table so hard that when she got up, it almost tumbled over. "How dare you talk to me like that!"

Just as I was about to make sure Aunt Maxi wouldn't leap across her table to try to get to Bunny's throat, the bell over the door dinged.

"Welcome to the Bean Hive." Bunny's disposition turned on a dime. She planted a big smile on her face and stood up. Just as pleased as a peach, which I was sure was because she'd gotten the last word in.

She and Aunt Maxi knew I wouldn't stand for their bickering while there was a customer.

CHAPTER TWO

$\mathcal{T}$he morning rush came and went, and so did Aunt Maxi's rant. I assumed she got tired of waiting for Bunny to make a comeback at her, so she sat at one of the café tables sipping her coffee and talking to everyone coming in and out the coffee shop door. That didn't mean she was finished with Bunny. It meant she would be able to get her wits about her and come back for seconds.

Bunny knew it too.

Bunny was good at talking to the customers, though she was a tad bit slow on getting them their orders ready. They didn't seem to mind. In fact, I think customers liked Bunny waiting on them. She was sort of the grandmother type that gave advice when you didn't want it. Well meaning, she was, but still, she'd tell a customer they needed to get two muffins instead of one because they were too skinny... those types of comments.

I'd just gotten finished cleaning up the coffee station when Louise Carlton walked through the door with a cat carrier in hand and a folder underneath her arm. She looked so well put together with her silver bob hair nicely curled under. Her bangs were perfectly cut above her brows. She was such a beautiful middle-aged woman.

"I can't wait to meet our new friend." My eyes focused on the carrier that was a little too small to hold a dog, and Louise didn't seem to be having any trouble holding it until Pepper came running up to get a good whiff of the new furry friend she had brought.

"A beautiful cat." Louise lifted the carrier for me to peer inside. The bracelets on her wrists jingled. The big jeweled ring on her finger twinkled under the coffee shop lights.

"Hey there." The poor baby was as huddled in the back as far as it could be. The eyes' black pupils were the size of marbles. I slowly blinked a few times like Louise had taught me to do with the cats when I became a volunteer at the Pet Palace a long time ago.

Louise claimed it was a way for the cats to get a hug from you and to tell them you are nice or safe.

"What's the story?" I asked Louise. I motioned for her to follow me back to the counter where I'd display all of the cat's information and Louise's business card to attract potential fur-ever homes for the cat.

"A stray. A hunter found her and brought her into Pet Palace. She's been looked over by the vet and given the shots and has been cleared for adoption." Louise set the carrier on the floor of the coffee shop.

While she opened the folder, I made her a cup of coffee she could take with her and slipped a couple of coffee soufflés in a to-go bag. I knew she loved them, and I knew they'd be gone before we turned around. They were already selling like hotcakes.

"Mornin'," Perry Zella said, waving from the front of the coffee shop. A couple of his mystery club members had followed him inside. They had started meeting at the Bean Hive once a month for the past four months to discuss different unsolved mysteries and various mystery books they were reading.

I really enjoyed having them there because they loved to question me about the legality of everything, since I was a lawyer by trade and a coffee shop owner by heart.

"Good morning! I'll bring y'all a carafe in a second." I placed Louise's to-go items on the counter in exchange for the paperwork. "What is the cat's name?" I asked Louise.

"There is no name." She frowned. I could tell her heart was hurting as much as mine at the thought that this little baby had been outside in the woods, cold, hungry, and probably scared. "Why don't you name her?" Louise's eyes lit up at her idea.

"She is brown and tan." I couldn't help but notice she was probably a mix of different breeds because she didn't resemble any sort of breed I'd ever seen. "What about Mocha?"

"Perfect." Louise clapped her hands together and bent down. "Now, Mocha, you be a very good girl, and Pepper will love you so much," Louise told Mocha while I turned to the coffee pots behind me to start a carafe for Perry and his mystery friends.

"I'm sure we will be great." I wiped my hands down my apron and walked around the counter to get Mocha's cage so Louise could leave with peace of mind. "Why don't we put her on the cat tree and see how she does."

It wasn't really a question. Patrick had built a cat tree for the cats because when Sassy was around, she knew no boundaries with other animals and wanted to play with them all, so his solution was to make a nice tall cat tree that let them hide from Sassy. It worked pretty well too.

"Since Sassy isn't here yet"—I picked up Mocha's cage—"I'll let you know how she adjusts," I said to Louise and walked her toward the door on my way to the cat tree.

Louise had stopped to talk to Aunt Maxi on the way out. I heard Aunt Maxi telling Louise how Loretta Bebe had given her the lead part in the winter theater production put on by the community theater. Bunny let out a few huffs from across the room, showing her disapproval of how Aunt Maxi's already-inflated ego had gotten bigger. Or at least that was how I read Bunny's body language.

"Now." I lifted the cat carrier to the very top of the cat tree shelf and peered in at Mocha. "You are going to be so happy when you realize that you're going to have a magnificent family home here in Honey Springs."

I put the cage on the top and bent down to open the small door, a little box Patrick had built into the cat tree where I could store various cat toys and treats.

I grabbed a couple of the treats and opened the cage door, and I placed the treats right outside of it.

"You can come out whenever you want." I gave Mocha a couple of slower blinks and resisted putting my hand into the cage to try to pat her. She still had that scared look, and her pupils appeared to have gotten bigger. "Let's go, Pepper. You need to give her time."

Pepper was so good. He acted like he understood exactly what I was saying, and we headed back to the counter to get Perry's coffee for the group. Pepper followed me all over the coffee shop, but I noticed him stopping a few times to look at the cat tree in anticipation of running over and doing his usual greeting of smelling, sniffing, and licking. He might be surprised and get a claw.

"What are y'all discussing this week?" I asked Perry and set down the tray of mugs along with the sugars, creamers, and honey for the guests to use as they pleased.

"It's been quiet in the Kentucky mystery scene, and it's pretty slow right after the holiday, but we are sure it's going to pick up sometime soon. So we are having a little coffee and company this fine snowy morning." Perry smiled. The lines around his eyes deepened. His grey brows matched his short grey hair. "Maxine…" His smile grew bigger when he said her name. "I couldn't help but overhear you got the lead in the town theater production. Congratulations."

Aunt Maxi did something that I'd never heard her do before. A giggle. She giggled like a little girl.

"Oh, Perry." She blushed.

I looked at her with wide eyes and tried to wrap my head around the fact I was standing there, living and breathing, watching her flirt with Perry Zella.

"I honestly can't believe it. When Loretta called me to ask me to go through the formalities of auditioning but knew I was going to get the part, I was so honored." Aunt Maxi had put a hand on Perry's shoulder as she stood next to him.

"Well, I don't know anyone who could play a better dramatical part than you, Maxine Bloom." Perry Zella actually winked at Aunt Maxi while he patted her hand.

"Oh, Perry. You sure do know how to make a girl blush." She giggled again, patted him one more time, and then walked away with a big grin on her face.

"And what was that?" I asked her and looked under my brows toward Perry and his friends.

"She was making a fool of herself. That's what that was," Bunny said in a sarcastic tone and pointed at Aunt Maxi. "You ought to be ashamed of yourself, teasing Perry like that. He's a new widower and…"

"New widower, my foot. Carolyn has been dead for over two years now." Aunt Maxi gave Bunny the side-eye. "He's just ripe for the pickin'." She sighed. "And I'm going to ask him to come to see me at the play."

"Of course you are," Bunny snarled before she put a big fake smile on her face. "How can I help you today?" she asked the two women who walked up to the counter.

"Yes. I'm looking for a Loretta Bebe. I'm to have met her here about ten minutes ago." The older woman of the two wore a long fur coat that looked real and long beige leather gloves that appeared to go all the way to her elbows. She picked at the tips of each finger and then pulled the gloves off her hands before smacking them into the hands of the younger-looking woman.

"This is Gretchen Cannon." The young girl acted as though we knew who Gretchen Cannon was. The girl wore a simple black puff jacket, her hair pulled back into a ponytail, and glasses that were too big for her face.

Gretchen Cannon had short flaming-red hair, an orange coat, and the brightest orange-red lipstick I'd ever seen. The wrinkles around her eyes and her lips were caked in makeup where she'd tried to cover them. The red-rimmed glasses were so large on her face that they were hard not to stare at. It appeared she was much more of a larger-than-life person than Aunt Maxi. And that was saying something.

"Hi. This is Roxanne Bloom, the owner of the coffee shop." Bunny didn't let the two women intimidate her. I chuckled on the inside. "We want to know what you'd like to drink."

"I don't think you understand," The young girl pulled her shoulders back.

"Thar you arrr," Loretta Bebe said, drawing her words out in her southern accent. "I'm Low-retta Bebe, and you must be the actress Gretchen Cannon sent." She looked between the two ladies.

"Gretchen. Gretchen Cannon." The young girl pointed at Gretchen, as though Gretchen couldn't speak for herself.

I lifted my coffee mug to take a sip.

"Oh dear," Gretchen gasped in some sort of accent that told me she wasn't even from the United States, but it was lovely. Maybe England? Ireland? I wasn't good at placing dialect or tones.

Gretchen looked Loretta up and down. "Honey, you've got to stop going to the tanning bed."

I tried, I really tried to stop myself from laughing at Gretchen's observation of Loretta, but I couldn't. I exploded. The coffee sprang out of my mouth and watered Gretchen's face like a sprinkler.

"My stars!" Loretta gasped. "Get me a towel!"

Bunny sprang into action and got them a towel, while I profusely apologized for my actions.

Gretchen tried to bat Bunny's hand away because Bunny was going to town so hard I was afraid she would wipe off Gretchen's skin.

"Oh my." Bunny gasped and looked down as a set of Gretchen's false lashes fell on the ground like a limp spider.

"Oh." Loretta whimpered and wrung her hands.

"Here." Aunt Maxi chimed in and ripped the towel from Bunny. "I'm sorry. They are babbling buffoons. I'm Maxine Bloom." Aunt Maxi gingerly patted Gretchen's face with the towel before she handed it to the young woman with Gretchen.

"I'm Gretchen Cannon, the star of the local play." The woman's voice dripped with pride.

Aunt Maxi's face went through a few different emotions as she bit her lip, then turned to stare at Loretta.

"I... um..." Loretta bit her own lip. "I'll get right back with you, Maxine."

Me, Bunny and Aunt Maxi watched Low-retta nervously shuffle the two women to one of the café tables near the fireplace.

I tried not to laugh, but it started all over again.

"Did you hear what she said about Loretta's tanning?" I asked Bunny.

"I did. Wait until she finds out Low-retta is one hundred percent Cherokee," Bunny said sarcastically in her best Loretta accent, sounding the way Loretta did when she claimed she didn't go tanning and it was natural.

Naturally fake down to her short hair, which was dyed midnight black, and her long acrylic fingernails. In fact, when Loretta was at Lisa Stalh's house, using the tanning bed Lisa kept in her garage, Lisa was in the house getting her manicure set together. She did Loretta's nails, though she'd take all this to the grave. But knowing this was part of owning the only coffee shop in town.

People gossiped. I loved to joke that the gossip at the coffee shop was as hot as the coffee. Truly, no one was above the gossip, and something about everyone in Honey Springs had been gossiped about around here.

"Seriously. What was that?" Bunny asked. "I thought you got the lead part."

"I'm not sure, but I'm about to find out." Aunt Maxi grabbed a couple of mugs and a pot of coffee like she owned or even worked at the joint, hippity-hopping her way over to the women.

Bunny and I watched as the four women conversed, and then it happened. Aunt Maxi's face turned all sorts of colors before it landed on red. I mean bright red. And all the way down to her neck, which I knew had fallen on her chest, and eventually making it to her hands, where it'd leave blotches.

"She's gonna blow," I warned Bunny right before Aunt Maxi started to let out a giant-size hissy fit.

"Now, Maxine. You wount the best for our town, don't youuu?" No amount of southern charm Low-retta tried to throw on Aunt Maxi would stick. No amount. "Now, be a doll and listen to me." She patted Aunt Maxi on the arm, trying to steer her away from the woman Gretchen and the young girl.

While Loretta walked Aunt Maxi towards me, I noticed none of this bothered Gretchen. The girl was a bit flustered and trying to talk to Gretchen, who was sitting calmly with her hands perfectly folded in her lap.

"You said this was your production. You said this was local, and now you've got some big producer coming here to do our town play. Where are you getting the funds?" Aunt Maxi drew her arms around the room. "Look around, Low-retta! It's winter, and we have very few tourists this time of the year."

"You aren't listening, Maxine Bloom," Loretta tried to whisper and eyeball me at the same time.

I shrugged and let her deal with the mess she'd created.

"You are still in the play, but don't you want to be a big star?" Loretta's dark brows rose dramatically, as did the southern tone in her voice, making it appear as if what she was saying was more important than the actual demotion. "I've called in a favor from Alan Bogart."

"Who the dag-burn is Alan Bogart?" Aunt Maxi questioned and crossed her arms.

This little exchange was particularly interesting to me. First off, Aunt Maxi didn't shut down or fall for Loretta's obvious attempt to get her not to throw the giant-size hissy fit and see things clearly. Secondly, someone owed Loretta a favor.

Now that alone was something extraordinary. Loretta never let a favor go owed for any long period of time since I'd known her. Trust me when I said that Loretta had a lot of pull in Honey Springs, though we didn't let her know that directly.

Oh, she knew it. She had the big head to prove it, but we'd never let

17

her know that we knew. Regardless, I was all sorts of turned upside down to hear just exactly the favor this Alan Bogart owed her and who he was to our little local theater play.

"Why, Maxine Bloom," Loretta gushed. "A so-phist-i-cated woman like yourself doesn't know who Alan Bogart is?" The syllables in her words dragged out.

"Well, I know the name, but I'm so riled up I can't place it right now." Oh my, Aunt Maxi was so good at trying to lie her way through not accepting that she had no idea who this Alan Bogart was, and her idea was to blame it on being southern.

Something she was really good at.

"Of course," Loretta said with a pinched tone. A few beads of sweat formed on her upper lip. Loretta was a jumble of nerves inside but would never let it show on the outside. "I'm sorry seeing Gretchen Cannon, one of the best off-Broadway actresses, here to act alongside of you."

My eyes lowered as I looked at Loretta, knowing her game. Did she forget I had practiced law and could see right through her manipulation?

Ahem, Aunt Maxi cleared her throat when she heard the word "Broadway." I was certain she put the "off" part in the back of her memory.

"Max-een." Loretta's drawl was really strung out. "You are a star," she said with a widened mouth, ending in a smile. "You know Alan."

I could tell she was teasing Aunt Maxi because Aunt Maxi had no idea who Alan was, but Aunt Maxi would milk it for all she could.

"Yes. Alan is very… um… what is the word?" Aunt Maxi rolled her wrist as if she were trying to find the right words, but I knew better. It was her way of getting Loretta to finish the sentence without appearing she had no idea what Loretta was talking about.

"Motivated to make the best play possible, since he is a famous producer." Loretta's words caused Aunt Maxi to stiffen up.

Aunt Maxi drew her shoulders back and chin up, cocking her right brow.

"Yes, that's the word. Motivated." Aunt Maxi's gaze drifted ever so slightly to Gretchen Cannon. "I guess I could share the stage with Gretchen."

"You are so professional." Loretta let out a deep, gratified sigh.

The stress of Aunt Maxi had made Loretta sweat a little, which made her makeup slide off a smidgen and expose the white lines she desperately tried to cover that were created by the tanning goggles.

Loretta gave one last nervous smile before she turned and headed back to Gretchen and the young woman.

"She's on Broadway. Think of it." Aunt Maxi drew her hands in front of her like she saw her name on the marquee underneath the Broadway lights. "Maxine Bloom starring in the lead with Gretchen..." She snapped her fingers.

"Cannon." I helped her recall the actress's last name.

"Yes. With Gretchen Cannon as a supporting actress." Aunt Maxi's face softened as she looked out to the horizon. "I've got to make sure it says that at the theater," she commented as though visualizing exactly how the chalkboard outside of the local theater would look as well.

CHAPTER THREE

I'd like to say Aunt Maxi had continued with her dignified southern attitude, but the longer she sat at the counter and watched Loretta Bebe cater to Gretchen Cannon, the more her face twisted and turned like she'd been sucking on a dill pickle.

It wasn't until a peculiar-looking fellow walked into the shop that I saw Aunt Maxi's attitude shift from angry to curious.

"Who's that?" she muttered, watching his every move. "He looks like those artsy people. Another one of Low-retta's twists?"

I ignored her and greeted the gentleman when he walked up.

"Good morning." I smiled. "Can I help you?"

He had on one of those *go to hell* hats, or at least that was what we called them in the south. The kind that almost lay flat on the head with a little bill out in front. I think I'd seen actors from Ireland wear them. And he wore a nice brown canvas coat with shiny brown buttons and a corduroy collar.

"Yeah." He was too busy scanning the chalkboard menus above his head to notice me checking out his shoes.

Penny loafers. Shiny as the buttons on his coat.

"Get the chocolate souffle." Aunt Maxi took it as her in to get into a conversation with the man. "Roxy's special roast too. She has a small roaster in the back. She gets a big ol' bag of beans imported right from the grower. I don't mean any beans. High-dollar ones."

"Is that right?" The man smiled, his eyes dancing. The amusement of Aunt Maxi intrigued him. "You look like someone I ought to introduce myself to."

"I guess you ought," Aunt Maxi mocked, "if you want to know anything around Honey Springs because I know you ain't from here."

He laughed as Aunt Maxi kept on flapping her jaws.

"I'm Maxine Bloom. That there is my niece Roxanne Bloom." She pointed at me. "Now, she was a lawyer, but now she is making coffee like I told you, and she's married." Aunt Maxi rolled her eyes. "Get him a cup of coffee," she instructed me when I started to interrupt her about telling strangers my life.

His eyes shifted to me, and we both smiled.

"She should take her husband's last name, but she did that once, and well, she ain't married to him no more." I heard her telling my life story as I got him a cup of coffee.

"The condiments are over on the coffee bar if you need anything to doctor up the coffee." I gestured.

"Doctor up?" he questioned, giving me the same goofy grin he'd given Aunt Maxi.

"Creamer. Sugar. Things that don't make coffee coffee." I tried to cover my accent, but I wasn't an actress like Aunt Maxi was trying to be, and being myself was the only way I knew how to be.

"I gotcha." He gave a hard nod. "Just like it black."

That made me happy.

"Then you're going to love my special roast. How long are you visiting?" I asked and also took a vested interest in why he was here because he didn't look like our usual winter tourists who were here to do ice fishing and cold hiking through the woods.

"As long as the play has its run."

That made Aunt Maxi jump off the stool with joy.

"I'm the lead," she cried out. "Are you someone famous?"

"I'm a reviewer for the *Times*." The curious smile faded. His eyes held a question. "What do you mean you're the lead?"

"As in the *New York Times*?" The question gushed out of Aunt Maxi.

"Yes, ma'am." He picked up the coffee cup. "What do you mean lead? I thought Gretchen Cannon was the lead Alan Bogart had cast."

"Gretchen Cannon. Alan Bogart." Aunt Maxi snarled. "I've got to call Low-retta right now."

Aunt Maxi must've forgotten all about Mark and his *New York Times* gig, but I hadn't. Serving him up a piece of the chocolate soufflé would definitely get his palate moving and jaw flapping.

"Follow me." I moved around the counter and took him straight over to the table next to Perry Zella and his group of mystery club folks. "Perry, this is Mark Redding. He's here for the Times." I'd totally realized I never knew what he did, but I assumed he was here to do a piece on Honey Springs.

"I'm a theater reviewer and have covered many plays by Alan Bogart." Mark had a funny look on his face, one that told me he wasn't a big fan of Alan's. "I'm curious to see this small-town play when Alan is used to a little bigger."

"Oh. I know." I shrugged, giving a little bit of the gossip I'd heard earlier. "He owes Loretta Bebe a favor."

Perry laughed, as did the rest of his group.

"Oh boy, he must've really had Loretta do something to owe her a favor." Perry's brows lifted.

"Trust me when I say Alan Bogart doesn't do favors for just anyone, so I must meet Loretta Bebe." Mark sat down.

"Let me introduce you to my mystery club." Perry did exactly what I had planned when I'd picked the spot for Mark to sit. He'd taken Mark into the fold of the warm hospitality Honey Springs had to offer, now more important than ever.

Loretta wasn't the most welcoming citizen we had, but Perry and his friends would intrigue Mark.

"He does play reviews for the New York Times," I told Bunny Bowowski when she moseyed up to me to get the particulars on him.

"New York Times?" She drew her hand up to her chest. "That seems big time. Especially for our small theater."

"Mmmhmmm." I plated his soufflé and handed it to her. "You can find out all about it. I've got to get the lunch items started."

Leave it up to Bunny to sit down with Mark, where I knew she would pump him for all the information that would keep us in gossip until the end of the play's run, which I believed was two weeks. Or did I read that wrong in the Honey Springs newspaper? Either way, there was a story behind Loretta and this producer that I couldn't put in the back of my head.

Quickly I rushed through the coffee shop to clean up any dishes lying around, fluff the pillows on the couch, stoke the fire, and check on Mocha.

Her head was out of the cage, but her body was half in. Pepper was still in the bed up near the register where he took his morning nap. It was almost time for me to take him out to go potty and for our morning walk, so I made sure the tea and coffee stations were cleaned up and stocked before I took my apron off and slipped on my coat.

Pepper hopped to his feet when he heard me take the leash off the coat tree. He waited patiently while I put on his little coat and harness.

"We will be right back to start lunch," I told Bunny on my way past her.

Bunny was too busy talking, so she simply waved her hand in the air to let me know she heard me.

The boardwalk held fond memories for me, since I used to spend my summers here with my Aunt Maxi.

Pepper loved heading down the boardwalk and greeted people as he went. He knew he had to get to the grassy area in order to do his business.

All the shops were locally owned and pretty much boutique style. Wild and Whimsy was the first shop on the boardwalk. It was an eclectic shop of antiques and repurposed furniture. Beverly and Dan Teagarden were the owners. Their two grown children, Savannah and Melanie, helped them run it. Instead of installing a regular shingled roof, Dan had paid extra to put on a rusty tin roof to go with the store's theme. They'd kept the awning a red color but without the name. The Wild and Whimsy sign dangled down from the awning.

Honey Comb Salon & Spa was located next, and it was a fancy salon —for Honey Springs. Alice Dee Spicer was the owner, and from what I'd overheard through the gossip line, Alice had really gotten some new techniques from a fancy school.

Next to Honey Comb Salon & Spa was the Buzz In and Out Diner owned by James Farley. Bees Knees Bakery was next to the diner and owned by Emily Rich. All About the Details, an event center, was next to the bakery. A bridal shop, Queen for the Day, was right next to my shop, The Bean Hive.

The snow was still coming down, and it didn't appear to be stopping anytime soon. It was fine as long as the roads didn't get icy. The snow sure made for a pretty scene. The banners dangling from the lampposts had to have been the ones Bunny and Aunt Maxi couldn't agree on, but I'd bet it was safe to say it was the last thing on Aunt Maxi's mind.

Pepper did his usual sniffing around when we made it to the grassy area between the Cocoon Inn and the boat dock.

"Excuse me." I looked up when I heard someone walk up.

"Hi." I smiled when I noticed the young woman who'd been with Gretchen Cannon at the Bean Hive. "I'm sorry. I was just looking at all the boats in the slips with their covers on them. All tucked in for winter."

It fascinated me how Big Bib, the owner of the boat dock, was able to winterize so many boats. Though it didn't seem like a boat dock would be open during the winter months, Big Bib claimed this season was his busiest time of the year. He said repairing boats and slips was completed during the winter months because he didn't have anyone bothering him. I could see his point.

"Yeah, I don't know anything about those." She pushed her glasses up on her nose. "I'm Sydney O'Neil, Miss Cannon's personal assistant," she said in a stern voice.

Oh, so formal, I thought when she stuck her hand out for me to shake. An umbrella was attached at her wrist. A black bag hung from her shoulder.

"And Miss Cannon really enjoyed the coffee you gave her and would like to hire you to do the food service stand at the theater while she's in town."

Sydney put up the umbrella and handed it to me.

"Please hold this while I get out the schedule." She shoved it toward me, and out of reaction, I took it. She pulled the black bag around to her chest, stepped under the umbrella, and took out a piece of paper. "Miss Cannon doesn't like anything to be out of order, and if a single snowflake gets on this paper, she will not like it."

"That explains the umbrella," I said and wondered if Gretchen was hard to work for, since Sydney sure did make it seem that way.

"Among other things." Sydney relaxed a smidgen when she looked at me. "I guess I don't have to be buttoned up with you."

It was nice to see her jawline soften and a smile cross her lips.

"Why hello there," she said to Pepper when he ran up to us and sat next to her feet. "I saw you sleeping in the coffee shop."

"Sydney, this is Pepper." I always took pride in how good he was. He never jumped on people, though he did bark occasionally. He was a really good dog. "He is my constant companion."

"Gretchen is my constant companion," she said in a sarcastic tone. "Or maybe I'm hers."

"Sydney, I think you just made a joke." I laughed, and she smiled again.

"If you do decide to take the job to supply the coffee, I do have to warn you because you seem so nice." Her brows pinched. "She is very particular on how she likes things run, and coffee is one of those things." She handed me the piece of paper.

"I'm flattered she's asking for it." I wondered how hard it could be and then looked at the paper. "Oh dear. She wants me to be there early and a hot cup be brought to her dressing room." I bit my lip. "I don't think there are dressing rooms in the local theater."

I tried to think back to the last time I was in there and really couldn't recall.

"That's an issue." She took a pen from her bag and a notebook. "Call Loretta about the dressing room," she talked and wrote the reminder.

"Still, if there's no dressing room, I'm more than happy to supply the coffee but not sure if I can be there every day to hand her a hot cup." I didn't bother going into details on how I opened up, took the coffee to the Cocoon, then returned to the coffee shop to work the morning shift with Bunny. "I'm more than happy to give her a personal carafe for her room that'll keep warm all day even."

"I guess that'll be fine. She's just so used to getting what she wants." She pointed at another paragraph on this paper. "She'd like you to also bring over the maple pecan breakfast ring daily to have with the coffee."

"Maple pecan…" My mind drifted to what on earth we had in the glass counter that made her think it was a breakfast ring.

"She stopped at the Bees Knees Bakery on our way to check in at the Cocoon Hotel. That was where she had gotten it." She pointed at the paragraph underneath the demand for the breakfast ring. "It states here that you are to bring it with you daily."

"I'll have to check with Emily Rich on that." When I saw her frown, I knew she was confused. "Emily is the owner of the bakery, and she'd have to agree to make one of these daily for Gretchen."

"Miss Cannon," she corrected me. "She doesn't really like people she's not friends with calling her by her given name."

"I think I'll stick with calling her Gretchen if she wants my coffee." I wasn't going to bow down to some lady who appeared to be more washed up in her career than thriving.

"That's fine between me and you, but you've been forewarned if she bites you." Sydney seemed a tad bit frightened at the fact.

"I'm a big girl. I can take it, or I can take my coffee back." It wasn't a threat. It was a fact. I wasn't about to let Gretchen bully me. "In fact, I was a lawyer, and let me give you some free advice. If you don't like working for her, there are several more people out there who are nice and kind."

"I like working for her just fine." The buttoned-up Sydney O'Neil was back. "So if you agree to bringing the coffee and the carafe, please sign this paragraph so I have something to take back to her. Then please let me know what Emily Rich has to say about the maple pecan breakfast roll."

I signed the paper, and then she pulled a card from the pocket of her jacket and handed it to me.

"Can I ask you one thing?" I waited until I knew I had her attention. I handed her the umbrella back once the paper was safely back in her bag. Lord forbid the young girl get a tongue lashing from the old lady. "Exactly how did Gretchen Cannon get the role in the play?"

"Alan Bogart. She owed him a favor, and here we are."

"Gosh." I snorted. "Seems like everyone is collecting on favors."

"Huh?" she asked.

"Nothing." I tugged on Pepper's leash for him to stand. "Pepper and I have to get back to the coffee shop. Business never stops."

"Thank you, Roxanne." Sydney tried to seem personal, but it didn't appear to come naturally to her. Maybe it was too many years of putting up with someone as bossy as Gretchen Cannon.

"You're welcome." I almost told her to call me Roxy, but I only let my friends call me that, so I just let it be.

Besides, I couldn't wait to stop at the Bees Knees Bakery to taste this maple pecan breakfast ring. My mouth was already watering.

"Good morning," Emily Rich said in greeting when I walked into the bakery.

"Emily," I gushed and dropped Pepper's leash.

After she noticed he was with me, she grabbed one of the organic bakery treats she made for her fur customers and bent down to give it to Pepper.

"I've got to try this maple pecan breakfast ring."

"Roxy, you'll never believe it." She stood up and handed me a treat that I knew she meant for me to take to Sassy. "I made it by accident when I realized I'd forgotten to put the raisins in the raisin loaf. So I slapped on some maple glaze, and it's the best-selling thing I've ever made."

"I can't wait to try it." I looked over her shoulder to try to see the breakfast ring.

"I'm out." She shrugged. "When it slows down this afternoon, I'll make several more and maybe into the night."

"You're going to have to if you want to fulfill Gretchen Cannon's wishes." I snorted.

"The actress lady with all the orange on?" Emily asked. "Really, she shouldn't be wearing such a bright color. It ages her even more."

Emily cracked me up. At times she seemed so adult and others still the young, freshly turned twenty-year-old she was. Emily had worked for me in high school and used the kitchen to perfect her pastries. She tried to go to college to please her parents but didn't have the passion. It took a lot of coaxing on my end and talking to her parents to let them realize Emily had a dream that was very much in her grasp.

They ended up embracing their daughter's dream and let her fly off into the world, where she went overseas to pastry school and became a pastry chef. She ended up buying Odd Ink Tattoo Parlor on the board-walk after it became available and opened Bees Knees, making it very successful.

I was glad too because it allowed me to cut back on making pastries to go with my coffee.

"She loves your maple pecan breakfast ring." I watched Emily rush around the bakery. "She'd like to have you bake her a fresh one daily while the play is in its run, and I'm more than happy to take it to the theater for you because I am going to take the contract to provide the coffee every morning." I laughed. "You wouldn't believe the demands she wanted, but I made sure we didn't have to deal with the drama."

"Yes. Orange is not good." She sighed and grabbed some papers off the counter. Then she shuffled them together in a pile.

"Right," I said in a bland tone when I realized she'd not heard a word I'd said.

She stopped and looked at me. She put the papers on the counter and held them down with her hand as if they were going to blow away.

"I'm sorry. I'm not with it today." Her face softened, and she smiled. "Can you repeat that?"

"I was just saying the actress would like to order one of your maple pecan breakfast rings while she's in town. And I'll take it every morning along with the coffee," I said.

Emily's response really caught me off guard. Usually, Emily would be really happy to have a client, and she loved making the daily goodies for the Cocoon Hotel's hospitality room where all the guest could hang out and grab snacks. The Bean Hive provided a lot of coffee contracts to area businesses, and I always tried to bring Emily's bakery in on the deals if I could.

The bell over the bakery door dinged. We turned around. Pepper was so good that he stayed next to me even when the man smiled at him. Pepper knew eye contact and a smile as a visual cue to show off and get some pats out of it.

"Dwayne. You're early." Emily looked from me to the man, who looked very professional in his winter overcoat, black hat, and briefcase.

"Business is never early." Hearing his words and seeing his eyes roaming around the shop made me pause. "It looks like the place has good bones."

"Roxy, I'd love to provide whatever the actress needs. You said something about you taking it?" Emily was trying to distract my attention away from this Dwayne feller by talking fast and walking Pepper and me to the door.

"Yes… I …" I was going to finish my sentence, but she took a fur treat from her apron pocket and put it in Pepper's mouth.

"I'll have it ready for you in the morning." She practically shoved us out the door.

Pepper didn't seem to notice or mind how Emily had reacted. While he happily ate his treat, I lingered at the display window of the bakery and looked in at Emily and Dwayne, who was someone I'd never seen around these parts, which told me he wasn't a citizen of Honey Springs.

The two of them were looking at the papers Emily had gathered up and placed on the counter. Something very odd was definitely going on with Emily.

"She might think she can satisfy you with a treat," I told Pepper on our way back to the Bean Hive. "But it certainly doesn't satisfy my curiosity about whatever it is she's hiding."

CHAPTER FOUR

*I*f I thought I would have any peace when I got back to the coffee shop, I must've had a screw loose. Aunt Maxi and Loretta were still bickering back and forth about the roles and who was playing what.

"I just don't understand why you think you can bring some big celebrity in here like that without *con-versing* with the theater committee. I'm a pretty smart woman." Aunt Maxi tapped her temple. "Why don't you explain it to me, Low-retta?"

"Maxine, I do not need to do any explaining to you." Loretta picked at the edge of her short black hair and turned her chin away from Aunt Maxi, avoiding Aunt Maxi's glare. "The committee voted me as the one in charge, and I can do what I please."

"Not when it's not your money." Aunt Maxi had a point. "It belongs to the Southern Women's Club."

Oh my. I knew those were fighting words between the women.

The Southern Women's Club was a whole southern social society that the name explained without explaining. The club determined who was who in Honey Springs. When I was invited to join—yes, you had to be invited—I was happy to use the coffee shop's busyness as a great excuse not to have the time to participate and therefore give my special invite to someone else in the community.

"Who said I used any of the club's money?" Loretta's head spun around. Her eyes narrowed on Aunt Maxi's, her fake lashes leaving a shadow on her cheek. "As if it were any of your business, Maxine Bloom, but I was owed a favor, and since I'm the one in charge, I called in my favor."

There Loretta went again with the favor.

"What kind of favor have you of all people been holding on to?" Aunt Maxi asked exactly what I had been thinking.

"A long-ago favor, Max-een." Loretta rolled her eyes.

"Low-retta Bebe, I've known you all my God-given life, and as sure as I'm livin' and breathin', you cash in them favors before you can do the favor you're cashing in for." Aunt Maxi's eyes drew wide open. She pinched her lips together, and her brows drew way up on her forehead.

"Max-een, you don't know me as good as you think." Loretta was about to say something else when the door to the coffee shop opened and a man larger than life stepped in.

"I'm here," he sang out, making everyone in the coffee house look at him. "And there you are." His words must have dripped with honey because Loretta seemed to be stuck to them.

"Alan," she said, her voice humming a southern melody. "My dear, dear Alan. I've been waiting for you."

It was like watching some old black-and-white movie with all the formal chitchat and kissing on the cheeks as the two of them walked to the middle of the coffee house, where they embraced.

I looked around and noticed all eyes were on them, especially the eye of Mark Redding's camera. The smile on his face and the look in his eye told me there was something between him and Alan, whoever Alan was.

"What the hell are you doing here?" Alan's glare and Mark's expression told me everything I needed to know.

These two men didn't like each other.

"Now, now." Loretta's lips twitched in a nervous smile. "I see there is something going on here." She politely turned to Mark, clasping her hands in front of her. Her face pinched the southern smile, the type of smile that actually squished the entire chin up to the forehead with squinty eyes like a newborn baby. And I'm not talking a newborn a few minutes old. I'm talking a right-on-out-of-the-womb look.

"Uh-oh." Bunny moseyed up to me with the coffee pot in her grip. "I better get everyone's mugs filled up because Low-retta is about to have a dying-duck fit."

"Mmmmhmm," I agreed and kept my eye on the situation transpiring in front of me.

As if it couldn't get any better, Gretchen sashayed into the joint with Sydney rushing behind her. Gretchen peeled off her glasses and took notice of the situation at hand.

"Well, well. I came in here to find our fearless leader." Gretchen's words dripped out of her mouth like the pearl necklaces around her neck. She pointed a direct finger at Loretta. "And here I find my answer." Her finger moved from Loretta and slowly between the two men.

She quickly snapped that finger with another one. Apparently, that was Sydney's cue to take over. Sydney gave Gretchen a hand fan. While Gretchen pretended to be having some sort of her own personal summer, Sydney's soft voice grew louder as she talked.

"Miss Cannon didn't know exactly when Mr. Bogart was going to show up, since she is here to make good on her favor to him." Sydney gestured to Gretchen. "Miss Cannon has a very tight schedule where she needs to get back to Broadway before the next run of her show starts."

"You mean off-Broadway to the show that hasn't sold one ticket since the opening?" Mark asked with a snicker under his breath.

"And secondly, we would like to call the police to have an escort for Miss Cannon because we read online how Mr. Redding was here to do a review, and Miss Cannon does fear for her life with him around, since he is trying to destroy her career." Sydney made an awfully bold statement.

"Now, just you wait a minute. Just because your play isn't a real play and I wrote an honest review doesn't mean I destroyed your career." Mark looked past Sydney.

"I agree. I don't want him anywhere near my play," Alan demanded and looked at Loretta. "And what do you intend to do about this?"

"Alan…" Loretta fluttered her eyes.

"If she flutters those eyes any faster, she's gonna start a windstorm." Aunt Maxi was having too much fun watching Loretta squirm.

"Hi," I interrupted, feeling like I needed to step in. I gave a slight wave to all parties involved. "I'm Roxanne Bloom. I own the coffee shop, and I'm so glad you're here. But I'm not sure if you want to air your business in front of all the customers."

"Of course they do." Mark folded his arms and sat back in his chair. Perry and his mystery club friends seemed to really enjoy the interaction playing out in front of us. "This is how they create drama and get people to show up at their pitiful shows. They've been practically shoved out of off-Broadway, and I couldn't resist the urge to show up here to see exactly how they ruin your small community theater."

"We will not stand for this!" Sydney spat before she hurried out of the coffee shop behind a cursing Gretchen Cannon.

"I'm not sure who will pay for this," Gretchen hollered as she went out the door. "But someone will!"

Loretta looked as if she'd swallowed a possum. Even the tan dripped right off her face as she stood there stunned.

"You fix this." Alan pointed at Loretta. "No favor is worth him. Do you understand?"

Alan also walked out, leaving Loretta stammering. She threw a look at me before she stomped over my way.

"Roxanne, don't just stand there." She jutted her finger toward Mark. The jewels glistened, causing little specks of light to dance along the ceiling. "Do something!" she demanded.

"Everyone," I proclaimed. Then I did something. "Free coffee on me!" I looked at Loretta.

A shadow passed over her face, darkening her features. Or maybe the color was coming back. Either way, she was on fire, and as she took off out of the coffee shop, I knew the wrath of Loretta Bebe had been bestowed upon me.

She slammed the front door of the coffee shop, rattling the glass windows. I turned on my heels to head back to the counter, where Aunt Maxi and Bunny were huddled together. The chatter of the coffee shop picked up and made me feel better.

"Oh my dear. This is going to be the talk of the town." Bunny and Aunt Maxi had sidled up to each other.

"I know. I can't wait to get to the theater tomorrow to get the lowdown." Aunt Maxi, again, was having too much fun.

"You two stop that gossiping. If what the reviewer said is true, I don't want them to ruin our local theater with a bad show." The concern was real. Loretta had flaws, but when she did something, she did it with the full intention of making it perfect.

"Honey, we ain't gossiping." Aunt Maxi winked at Bunny as she spoke to me.

"No, dear." Bunny shook her head. "We are discussing prayer concerns."

"Is that what we are calling it nowadays?" I questioned and grabbed a carafe for each hand. I walked off, letting the two of them beat the situation until it was dead, then pick it up to beat it even more to make sure it was dead.

CHAPTER FIVE

I'd never seen the likes. It always amazed me how gossip spread around Honey Springs like melted butter on a hot biscuit. Before I could even get people's free coffee for them, the phone was already ringing off the hook from people trying to figure out what on earth had happened.

"You can tell all your customers to get online this afternoon and begin reading my article on my stay here in Honey Springs." Mark Redding seemed awfully happy about what he had in mind for his piece today.

I carefully formulated the words in my head as I filled up all the mugs on the table.

"I'm not so sure if painting a picture of Honey Springs as volatile would show what our town is really about." I shrugged in hopes of getting him to change his mind.

"Oh, you and the town folk will be fine. It's Gretchen Cannon and Alan Bogart who will bring a halt to your town production. Have you read the play?" he asked me. There seemed to be a truly concerned look on his face. "I can tell you haven't."

He bent down and opened his briefcase up. He took out a stack of papers and handed them to me.

"You read this for yourself. You'll see just how they no longer have what it takes to bring a show, even a small-town show, to life. They don't like me because I give an honest review. Anytime a big name goes into a small town, we get so many readers. Usually, those big names do things to help around the community or give back in some way." He snickered. "When my boss told me they were coming here, together, I knew I had to cover it. The only thing they give back is a hard time. When they are together, there's nothing but trouble that comes out of it."

He took a newspaper out of his briefcase.

"Here. Check out this article I did before I got here. It's all the ways they singlehandedly ruined the careers of actors and actresses who thought they had an opportunity in these plays that were either produced by Alan Bogart or Gretchen Cannon starred in."

I took the paper from him.

"You know…" Perry's brows winged up. "There's not much happening in Honey Springs this time of the year. It might be fun to watch all this play out. Maybe our mystery group should focus on the play, since we don't have a reading pick this month."

I shook my head and headed back to the counter. The last thing Loretta needed was a handful of people hanging around the theater and putting in their two cents or just being nosey.

Pepper started to potty dance around my feet when I put the coffee carafe back in its place.

"Time to go potty?" I asked Pepper.

The tips of his ears perked up, and his little tail wiggled back and forth.

"Perfect timing." I patted him on his head. I untied the apron from around my waist and hung it on the coat tree next to the counter, and then I grabbed Pepper's leash. Taking him outside would also get me out of the coffee shop for some fresh air and regrouping.

"I'm leaving too." Aunt Maxi grabbed her coat off the coat rack. "You let me know if anything happens," she told Bunny as if they were instantly best friends. A deadly combination.

37

"Oh, I will." Bunny nodded and headed back to take care of the customers at the counter.

"Nothing like good gossip to bring a town together," I told Aunt Maxi on our way out the door and noticed Mocha was halfway out of her cage.

She was getting more and more used to being in the coffee shop. It was the normal progression with cats, and I wouldn't be surprised if after the morning coffee rush died down, she ventured out of the cage and sniffed around.

"It's not gossip." Aunt Maxi turned left once we walked out the door to head over to the parking lot on that side of the boardwalk. "It's about being informed. I'm going to the theater to learn my new lines now that I'm playing a different role."

"You seem to be okay with that." I was curious about how she went from being upset about losing the starring role to being happy with a role that was secondary if that.

"I'm going to see how all this plays out," she said as calmly as could be. "Don't count me out yet." She gave me a theatrical wink. With a giddy-up in her step, she bolted off in the opposite direction from Pepper and me.

With the snow starting to fall a little harder, I wanted to make sure I kept an eye on the weather report. If the roads started to get a little icy, there was no sense in keeping the coffee shop open. It wasn't worth the risk to put Bunny or my afternoon high school employees at risk.

All the shops were still open, from what I could tell when Pepper and I passed on our way to the grassy spot. He quickly did what he wanted to do and got ready to get back to the coffee shop, where it was nice and warm.

A loud knock on the Wild and Whimsy display window made my heart jump as we passed.

Loretta Bebe was standing inside of the antique shop, flailing her hand for me to come in. I could see Alan, Gretchen, and Sydney were in there, talking to Dan and Beverly Teagarden. For a second I thought of waving as if she were waving at me, but like Mocha, I was curious and half tempted to go inside to see what they were doing.

It took only one more of Loretta's hand gestures to coax me from out of the cold. Within seconds, Pepper and I were standing next to her.

"I was going to come back down there and let you know what is what." Loretta's face was crimson with fury. "I'm telling you, that reviewer needs to leave, and if you keep welcoming people like him with open arms, he will ruin the play for sure, just like he said these two amazing Broadway talents predicted."

"Loretta, I know you are passionate about his play, but do we really need two people such as them to even put on a small-town play?" I asked, trying to bring my lawyer reasoning skills to life. "I understand your precious name is on the chalkboard outside of the downtown theater and you take pride in what you do, but when you have big people such as those two, it also comes with big headaches."

"Of all people in Honey Springs," she scoffed, "I figured you, Roxanne Bloom, were the most sophisticated and would understand my position."

"I'm not saying I don't understand your position." I wasn't going to let Loretta's sucking up to me sway me from what I felt was something she'd taken too far. "But I'm asking you to think about it. Think about the good of the town. Mark Redding has as much right to be in Honey Springs as those three."

Loretta and I looked over at the group. It appeared as if Alan were picking out props for the play and Gretchen was agreeing to things. Sydney wrote profusely as they talked.

Loretta continued to fuss underneath her breath but abruptly stopped when Sydney began to walk our way.

"Put a smile on your face." Loretta had forgotten somehow that she was not Aunt Maxi because that was something Aunt Maxi would say and had said to me in the past. That directive was generally followed up by the statement that I could have put on a little lipstick.

I did. I put a big smile on my face.

"I'm so glad you are here. It saves me from coming to the coffee shop to find you." Sydney pushed her glasses up on her nose. "Miss Cannon would like you to go on down to the theater to get a feel for exactly where you'll be putting the coffee stand along with the pastries so we do not have to spend any time walking around trying to figure out where you put it. Also, we'd like confirmation that you know exactly where Miss Cannon's dressing room is located so you won't be delayed in placing the coffee carafe in there and be ready for her six a.m. arrival."

"Six a.m.?" Loretta drew back. "Why, honey, my eyes are barely open at six a.m."

"Then I guess it's a good thing you aren't on stage." Sydney's comeback threw Loretta off her rocker and me for a loop.

Not until Sydney was out of earshot did Loretta start in on the poor girl.

"That girl is wound tighter than a girdle at a Baptist potluck." Loretta was back to her snide remarks, and I couldn't help but smile.

In fact, the smile stayed on my face until I walked back into the coffee shop.

"Hey." Patrick's face lit up when he saw Pepper and me walk in. "You look happy even after what Bunny just told me about what happened here."

It was nice to see the shop had cleared, leaving a couple of guests sitting on the couches, enjoying the fire and a cup of coffee.

"This smile is about the exact same situation." I gave my husband a kiss and patted Sassy on the head. She and Pepper were busy greeting each other. "I'll have to tell you all about it later."

"I came here to grab Pepper from you. I'm going home. It's slow this afternoon with the weather, so the less you have to deal with, the better." He was always thinking about the good of our little family. "Do you think you'll stay open?"

"I'm not sure. I was thinking about the weather when I was stopped by Loretta and the crew about making sure my coffee station was exactly where it needed to be and how I can't hold up the famous Miss Cannon." I did a dramatic bow like she was the queen or something.

"Oh no." Patrick took Pepper's leash from me. "I can see this is going to be very interesting."

"Nah." I shook it off. "It'll all work out fine. In the meantime, I'm going to check the weather, let Bunny go home, and then stop by the theater on my way home."

"Perfect. Sounds like a plan." Patrick gave me one last kiss, and I gave the pups a last kiss before they headed out into the snowstorm.

Turmoil was brewing in the air. I could feel it. I wasn't sure whether it was about the situation with Loretta and Alan Bogart changing Loretta's lead actress or the situation between Alan and Mark Redding, but something was about to blow up along with the snowstorm about to hit.

"Patrick is right about me needing to watch the weather," I told Bunny while she was refilling the freshly baked cookies on the tray in the display case. I grabbed the remote control for the small TV we had above the fireplace and turned the television on. "The banner on the screen says it's still coming our way."

Bunny and I both stopped what we were doing and read the ticker at the bottom of the television screen.

"Right now is the best it's going to get." I was talking about the weather and noticed the snowflakes were getting bigger and covering more space. The bottom of the television screen said the temperature was in the mid-twenties, which was plenty cold for the snow to stick and make things a little messy.

"Why don't you go on home?" I suggested to Bunny. "I'll get things buttoned up here and text the afternoon staff to let them know we will be closing early and not to come in."

"I don't want to leave you in a lurch. Are you sure?" Bunny asked.

"Yes, ma'am, I'm positive. I've got to make some pecan cookies for Loretta, and I'll head over to get a look at the theater before heading home to spend a free evening with my husband and fur babies."

"If you're sure." Bunny had already gotten on her pillbox hat and her gloves, but she was just being polite, as we all did.

"I'll call you in the morning if things change for tomorrow." I waved her on out, and she didn't hesitate. "It's just me and you, Mocha," I told the sweet feline who was still huddled in her cage on the very top rung of the cat tree.

Something about her was so sweet and endearing. She was definitely shy, and I truly wondered how she got here. I knew that if I kept talking to her like I did the other animals, she'd venture out even more as the week dragged on.

"I guess it was a bad week to come here." I talked to her as I propped open the swinging door between the kitchen and coffee shop. While I walked and talked, I quickly pulled my phone from my back pocket and sent a text to the afternoon staff to let them know I'd rather they be safe and at home instead of coming in with the big snowstorm on the horizon.

"The snow and of course the crazy theater stuff, it sure can get loud in this small coffee shop." I continued to talk out loud to Mocha and slipped the phone back in my pocket.

On my way over to the dry ingredients shelf to fetch the pecans I needed to make the pecan ball cookies, I checked the oven to make sure it was not only on but also set to the three-hundred-and-twenty-five-degree temperature needed to bake the cookies to perfection.

I emptied out the full glass jar of pecans, which were probably too many, but what good was a pecan cookie if it wasn't full of the nut?

"I'm going to use the chopper now." I leaned a little to the right and peered out the swinging door where I could see the cat tree in full view. "Mocha?" I questioned when I noticed she wasn't sticking halfway out of the cage.

A squeak of a meow caught my ear. I looked down and saw the sweet feline had made her way into the kitchen and squatted underneath Bunny's stool, which was butted up against the preparation counter.

"Hey there." I greeted her with a smile and blinked my eyes slowly a couple of times to let her know I was friendly. "You aren't going to like this chopping noise."

Using my hand, I gathered pecans into a pile before placing the chopping machine over top of the mound.

"Normally, I'd chop these up with my knife, but I'm being lazy and in a bit of a hurry to beat the storm this afternoon, so cheating with a chopper is what we are doing." I reached underneath the counter and grabbed the chopper off one of the open shelves.

After pounding out a few chops, I looked to see whether Mocha had stayed or run off. To my delight, she was still crouched there, but her eyes were wide open.

"What if I gave you one of these?" For her courage in staying there and venturing out, I unscrewed the lid of the mason jar of homemade cat treats that I made for my cat-owning customers. Of course I had dog treats, too, but today, Mocha and I were going to worry about the cat treats.

I took one of the fish-shaped treats out and placed it on the floor. "You are going to love my special fur treats." I watched to make sure she ate it before I put a few more on the ground.

The little fish treat crunched in between her small teeth. I took a few more out and put them next to her before I went on with making the pecan balls.

"I knew you'd love those salmon treats. And they are good for you." I was pretty proud that the three ingredients I used were organic. The salmon was from the local butcher, the eggs were from Hill's Orchard, and the flour was organic and gluten free. They were all good for Mocha, and her loud purring told me she enjoyed them.

"I'm expecting you to come out tomorrow and engage with the people. You deserve a good home." I walked over to the refrigerator and pulled out the butter and vanilla, and on the way past the dry ingredients shelf, I grabbed the sugar and flour.

I glanced down at Mocha, but she was gone. I didn't bother looking for her because I knew she was simply doing the cat thing of exploring her environment while no one was around. Something I was sure she'd be doing all night after I locked up for the evening.

Quickly I combined all the ingredients but the powdered sugar and rolled several dozen balls from the dough before placing them into the oven.

The fresh Columbian beans needed to be roasted, so I grabbed the coffee bag that was imported from Honduras. It was one of the freshest bags of beans I'd ever gotten. They were hand-picked using the dry method, which was why the bag cost me so much.

I headed over to the small roaster I had in the corner of the kitchen, reached into the burlap bag, and scooped up about a pound of the light-brown coffee beans. I carefully dumped the beans into the loading hopper so I didn't drop any on the floor, with the roasting temperature set to three hundred and ninety-two degrees.

I flipped on the fan, which caused the fan in the cooling bin agitator to turn on as the arms of the fan circled. They waited for me to open the bean release lever, which would release the freshly roasted beans. I watched the coffee beans through the small window as they rolled around in the drum and couldn't help but think that each one of those coffee beans was handpicked using the dry method. I pondered all of what went into the process.

It was an age-old method of processing coffee and still used in many countries where water resources are limited. The beans were actually called cherries that were freshly picked and spread out on huge surfaces to dry in the sun.

Every day they racked the beans so the beans wouldn't spoil. Then the people covered them at night or in rainfall to keep them from getting wet.

This particular bean was produced in Honduras, so it would take the beans a few weeks for the moisture in them to drop to the 11 percent needed before the beans actually started to shrivel and look like the coffee beans I was watching in the roaster.

"Too bad my roaster isn't bigger." I talked to Mocha as if she could hear me all the way out into the coffee shop. "If I had a bigger roaster, I could do several pounds of fresh coffee."

Even though I knew the roaster hadn't reached the peak temperature, I pulled out the sample spoon on the roaster. It was a long steel piece with a canal down the middle in which I could pull out a collection of the coffee beans. The sample spoon allowed me to look at the coloring of the beans, since the roaster took the beans from a light brown to a nice rich dark brown but did not burn them. It was a very precise process and one I didn't like to mess up.

I pulled the sample spoon up to my nose and took in the aroma of the warm beans. It was a smell like no other. Not even a fresh pot of coffee smelled this good, though that smelled good too.

Quickly I replaced the spoon when I heard a noise from the coffee shop.

"What are you doing?" I wiped my hands down my apron and walked into the coffee shop to see what Mocha had gotten into. I was delightfully surprised to find it was actually Emily Rich standing in the middle of the shop with Mocha in her arms.

"Hi!" I was happy to have a human there and happier to see Mocha in her arms. "You found Mocha."

"Mocha, how adorable." Emily laughed and ran her hand down the cat's fur. Then she put Mocha back down on the ground.

"You must be the cat whisperer."

Mocha started to rub her side up against Emily's leg.

"Mocha has been hiding in her cage all day."

"She's really sweet. I love cats." Emily gazed down at Mocha and then looked back to me.

"What's wrong?" I hurried over to Emily, wiping the final pecan ball mixture off my hands so I could comfort her. "What's with the tears?"

"I'm not sure how to tell you this because you've been so instrumental in my career and life." Her voice cracked as the words tumbled out of her mouth, and the tears fell in big drops down her face.

"Are you sick?" I asked, hoping to help her tell me whatever it was she needed to get out.

She shook her head.

"Is someone in your family ill?" I asked since I knew her family well.

"Just let me get this out." She sucked in a deep breath and pinched her lips as if doing that turned the tear nozzle off. "When I walked in here while I was in high school, I just needed a summer job because my dad made me. Then I realized how much I loved the baking part. You talked my parents into giving up their dream of me going to college, then off to Paris I went." The smile radiated from her as she spoke fondly of the past. "Then I came back, and you helped me open Bees Knees Bakery. My dream was to open a bakery right here in Honey Springs."

I wasn't sure what was coming, though my gut told me Emily had some big news that would forever change not only me but her.

"Owning a business hasn't been easy. Especially in a small town like Honey Springs. Over the past year, I've come to realize how much more I love baking than being the owner of a shop. The business side I'm not good at." She shook her head and rolled her eyes. "My dad even took over about nine months ago since I wasn't even good at balancing the checkbook, but I still love to bake."

"Are you shutting down the bakery?" I blurted out with a cry of disbelief. "I can help you with the books."

"See, this is why you are so well loved. You offer to help anyone with anything, always putting you and the coffee shop second and third." She reached out and grabbed my hands. "But I'm an adult, and I need to do what an adult does and make some big-girl decisions. That's why I've decided to take a position as the head pastry chef at another bakery that's in southern Kentucky."

"You're moving?" My jaw dropped. I did not expect her to tell me she was shutting down the bakery, but for her to actually move a few hours away was downright shocking. I really did try to put on a happy face for Emily, but my head was having a hard time wrapping around what she was saying. "Leave Honey Springs? Close the bakery?"

"I was afraid of this." Emily's brows dipped. She gnawed on the edge of her lip.

"Afraid of what?" I asked her. Though I was only thirty, I had to remind myself that Emily was still very young and just entering her twenties. I didn't want to hurt her feelings, and by the look on her face, she was upset.

"How you'd take the news?" She swallowed hard. "I'm forever grateful for everything you've done for me, and it's not that I've taken it for granted."

"Okay, stop." I walked over to her and wrapped my arms around her for a comforting hug. "I'm not upset at all. I'm sad because I won't see you on a regular basis, but I also know that you need to spread your wings and grow. I'm so happy for you and super-supportive."

"Oh, Roxy," she gushed and hugged me tighter. We stayed like that for a couple of seconds longer. We let go. "I do think it's best. Like I said, I was losing the passion for baking because all the business things had me tied up, and then after I'd take care of those things, all my creative baking energy was zapped. I was struggling to do all the things."

"Trust me, I understand." Not that I wanted to make this conversation about me, but I felt like I needed to remind her of my past. "Remember, I spent all the money on law school and opened up my own firm with my now-ex-husband, only to come here to start my passion, where I'm so happy."

"And that's what I kept thinking about when I was feeling disheartened. I knew you had decided to leave your big lawyer job behind, not that people here don't always hit you up." She joked, but she was right.

Even though I wasn't practicing in a law office, somehow citizens knew I still had my certified law degree, which I did make sure I kept current, and would ask me to look in or help with various things. Just because of my nature to serve people—and, these days, coffee—of course I helped them if I could.

"What are you going to do with the building?" I asked.

"I don't know." She shrugged. "I know it's a bad time of the year to even think about putting it up for sale, but I've got to be there next week."

"Next week?" My jaw dropped, and my eyes popped open. "Wow, that's soon."

"Soon to you, but honestly…" She hesitated and looked down at Mocha rubbing up against her. "I've been working on this for months.

The guy you saw in the bakery is buying all my equipment and inventory, which he's taking in a couple of days." She put her hands out in front of her. "Don't worry. I'll have all the pecan rings ready for you to take to the theater."

"I'm not even thinking about that." I shook my head and rolled my eyes. "Who knows if the show will go on?" I teased. "They are all about to implode with all the inner fighting. But I appreciate you getting those made."

I motioned for her to follow me back to the kitchen.

"I'm roasting some beans and don't want them to burn," I told her over my shoulder.

"I miss watching them spin," she whined on our way into the kitchen. "And I see you still haven't gotten a bigger one."

"Did I complain that much?" I asked her as we both noticed the temperature was about to reach the three-hundred-and-ninety-two-degree mark.

Just like old times, Emily, without me asking, turned the bean release lever just as the temperature was perfect.

"My favorite," she squealed as the dark-brown roasted beans fell out of the chute into the cooling tray, allowing the fan blades to circulate the beans while they cooled.

"I wish I had more space for a bigger one, but I don't," I told her as we both watched the beans being turned over and over and looked for any white beans.

"Found one!" Emily reached in and grabbed the white bean before the blades of the fan swept past and covered it up. "I'm putting it in my pocket."

"It still amazes me how some of the beans just don't get roasted." I laughed and remembered how Emily and I made a game out of who could find the most white beans after a roast. "Even though we haven't done this in a long time," I said, referring to us sitting there watching the roaster, "I'm sure going to miss seeing your face. But I'm incredibly proud of the woman you have become and are becoming. It took me well into my twenties to even consider going for what I wanted most in the world."

"You have no idea what that means to me." Her shoulders lifted to the bottoms of her ears, and a smile curled on her lips. "I have a great idea."

"Oh yeah?" I asked and started to scoop the full beans into Bean Hive coffee bags so customers could purchase them and take them home to grind. I also made sure to keep some back for me to grind so I could take them with me to the theater on my way home.

"Why don't you buy my building?" Her eyes lit up like the snow did in the sunlight.

"I don't want to be a baker." I laughed and headed over to the grinder.

"No, put a roastery in there. It would be great. You can give roastery tours. I've seen it in other cities." Emily nodded her head so fast that she looked like a bobblehead doll. "You can hold classes. It'll be great!"

"You know this all sounds good, but you are two shops down. It would be one thing if you were next door, but you're not." I hit the button for the grinder and talked over it. "Good idea, though."

"Think about it." She tapped the prep station with her fingertips. "I've got to go finish those pecan rings and make a few stops."

"How long do we have?" I asked.

"Less than a week." She frowned, but I could tell she was excited about her new adventure.

"Then all of us gals have to get together." I was referring to Crissy Lane, Camey Montgomery, Fiona Rosone, Joanne Stone, Kayla Noro, and Leslie Roarke. All of us were about the same age and hung out sometimes, and I knew they'd all want to get together to say goodbye to Emily.

"That would be great!" Emily brought her hands up to cover her mouth. "You're the first person I told, so I'm going to be heading on over to Crooked Cat now to tell Leslie, then to the Watershed to tell Fione."

Those must've been the few stops she'd referred to earlier.

Leslie was the owner of the Crooked Cat Bookstore on the far end of the boardwalk, and Fione was a waitress at the Watershed floating restaurant on Lake Honey Springs. The restaurant was located in front of Crooked Cat.

"You let them know I'll be texting them to get together." I gave Emily one last hug and noticed the snow was really piling up. "Now get out of here before we both get snowed in."

"I'll see you in the morning to pick up the pecan rings," she trilled on her way out the door. "Bye, Mocha!"

CHAPTER SIX

*T*he coffee turned out great. I went ahead and made two big carafes to take with me—one for the theater in case someone was there and one for home so Patrick and I could enjoy some coffee by the fire.

The roads were getting slick, and I made sure to drive pretty slow on the way into downtown Honey Springs, which was only a five-minute drive on a non-snowy day and a ten-minute drive today.

Downtown was a gorgeous small town. Central Park was smack dab in the middle of town. There was a sidewalk around it and different sidewalks leading to the middle of the park, where a big white gazebo stood. Most of Honey Springs's small-town festivals were held in the park. And I couldn't wait for spring to come back because I missed going to the farmers' market.

Dimly lit carriage lights dotting all the downtown sidewalks glowed and made a gorgeous picture with the falling snow. It was almost as pretty as the vivid memory of the colorful flowers and daffodils that I knew were hiding underneath the snow in the ground and would pop up soon to let us know spring was coming.

The courthouse was located in the middle of Main Street with a beautiful view of the park.

There was a medical building where the dentist, optometrist, podiatrist, and good old-fashioned medical doctors were located.

And the theater was near the library, which was across from the bank where Emily's dad was bank president.

Even the old theater looked great. It was a typical small-town theater with exposed light bulbs going all the way around the marquee, which was lit up on the top of the building. There were double doors and a small glass cashier window, where one of the members of the theater committee would sit and sell tickets for the show. The theater company did four shows a year, and those coincided with the seasons. Since we were still in the winter season, this was the winter show. With Loretta Bebe in charge of this one, I knew it was going to be over the top, just like her.

I made a U-turn in the middle of Main Street and parked in front of the theater. The street was empty, but the lights inside the theater were on, which told me someone was in there. I grabbed one of the coffee carafes and a plate of the warm pecan balls before I headed inside.

The Southern Women's Club took great pride in the theater. It was one of their works of philanthropy, and they made sure they did the necessary fundraising to keep the theater in the pristine shape it was in for its age.

They had replaced the long velvet red drapes along the wall with new velvet red drapes that were exact replicas of the originals. They also had the red carpet replaced to match the original carpet. The entrance was a long hallway that led right into the auditorium, where there were about fifty rows of seats with velvet covering the backs and bottoms. They were the originals and the most expensive to recover from what I remembered. But the Southern Women's Club did it.

The stage was the typical half-moon design, and there were two balcony box seats on both sides of the stage. Those were usually reserved for the mayor and other officials of Honey Springs.

I walked down the center aisle and headed to the left side of the stage, where the door led to the dressing rooms. I noticed Loretta had already put Gretchen's name on one of the doors, which made me happy because now I knew exactly where I needed to go in the morning with her sweet treat and special mug full of coffee.

Just in case she was in there, I gave a little knock before I opened the door.

"I'm sorry." I was shocked to find Alan Bogart, the director, in the room, standing over the makeup desk with the manuscript in his hands. "I... um..."

"What can I help you with?" He folded the manuscript and placed it under his arm.

"I was just making sure I knew where Gretchen's dressing room was before I showed up here in the morning with her requests from the coffee shop and bakery." I shrugged and noticed the briefcase lying on the makeup table was open and papers were spilling out of it.

"You found the right place. We are getting all the manuscripts to the actors before our morning rehearsal," he said with a stone face. "Did you happen to get rid of the reviewer?"

"You know, I live by the southern saying that I have no horse in that race, so that's something you're going to have to take up with him. But I am an expert on the weather around here, so you might want to get back to the Cocoon Hotel before it gets too slick to get back." I wanted to leave him with some friendly advice, but he didn't seem to be receptive to it.

"Are you also the weather girl?" he asked with a snide grin. "These little towns drive me nuts."

He pushed past me and out into the hall, leaving me at the door of the dressing room.

"I suggest you not be a half a second late in the morning, so you should watch the weather because Gretchen will eat you alive." He had turned around, walking backwards down the hall, giving me some advice with a huge smile on his face. "Better you than me." He let out a long, deep, evil laugh and turned around before he disappeared into the door that I knew led to the stage.

"Jerk," I muttered under my breath and took another quick look at the dressing room to see exactly where I would put the mug and pastry when I visited in the morning. Then I shut the door.

"That's ridiculous!" I heard the shrill voice of my aunt Maxi coming from inside the theater. "That is not what you told me!"

Oh man, someone was in trouble. I'd heard this tone from Aunt Maxi before, and I knew it was right before she threw a giant-sized hissy fit that no one wanted to see. Trust me.

Instead of just letting it go and her working it out so I could get in my car and get home to my little family, I sucked in a deep breath and prepared to head into battle—whatever battle she was griping about.

There she was standing on the stage in all her glory. Bleach-blond hair and all. If it weren't for her screaming and stomping, I would be shocked by the hair. I was used to all the different colors Aunt Maxi made her hair, but never had I seen her with short bleach-blond hair.

"Maxine…" Loretta Bebe danced around Aunt Maxi, using her pleading voice. "Alan is an award-winnin' producer. He knows what he's doing. I agree with you that it's a bit of a shock that we won't be doing the romance, but just think how much fun this little mystery will be."

"It's not the script, Low-retta," Aunt Maxi said with a growl. "It's the lead being taken away from me that I have an issue with. You asked me to be the lead. Not some dried-up actress."

"Well, Gretchen Cannon is dried up." Alan Bogart seemed to really be stoking the fire, the fire being Aunt Maxi.

"Who is calling who dried up?" Gretchen Cannon popped up from a chair in the front row.

"They can't possibly be talking about you, Miss Cannon." Sydney O'Neil jumped up to defend her employer.

"Nope." Aunt Maxi shook her finger directly at Gretchen. "I'm certainly talking about you. What was the last play you were in? Why are you here in Honey Springs? And you…" She turned her attention to Alan Bogart.

I squeezed my eyes closed in anticipation of what was going to come out of her mouth to help soften the blow to my ears.

"What kind of producer are you? One that doesn't take pride in his cleanliness, because I'm standing downwind of you and your stink is buckling my knees. And I'm sure Steven Spielberg doesn't stink." Aunt Maxi was on a roll. "Low-retta, you…"

"Now, Maxine…" Loretta had clasped her hands in front of her and was trying to calm down Aunt Maxi. "Why don't you sit a spell and simmer down."

"Simmer down?" Aunt Maxi raised a fist. "I'll show you how to simmer down."

"Hi!" I yelled from the back of the auditorium in hopes of stopping Aunt Maxi from taking up residence for the night in the Honey Springs sheriff's department. "What's going on?"

"There's my lawyer!" Aunt Maxi rushed over to the steps leading off the stage. She grabbed her coat and struggled with putting it on as she walked up the center aisle to meet me. "She'll get all this straightened out. Mark my words."

"Roxy, thank the Lord you are here." Loretta never praised me as such. "Can you talk some sense into your aunt?"

"Don't you listen to her," Aunt Maxi seethed through gritted teeth and slipped her hand into the crook of my elbow, guiding me toward the door. "She has lost all control of this production, and now those two have come in here and taken over." She turned around to face the group on stage. "I'm calling an emergency meeting of the Southern Women's Club. Do you hear me?"

Loretta let out an audible gasp. It was unheard of to call an emergency meeting with the Southern Women's Club and a tall threat when someone did.

"That'll give Low-retta something to chew on tonight." Aunt Maxi laughed. "Let's get out of here."

"Do you want to come to the cabin for some coffee and pecan balls?" I asked, knowing she needed someone to vent to and that I needed to talk her off the vindication I could see forming in her mind. "I know it's snowing and getting slick, but you got that truck."

"I'll meet you there." She gave a hard nod before she let go of my arm and started walking around the theater to the small neighborhood that was located behind the downtown business where she lived.

"Do you want me to drive you home to get your truck?" I asked.

"No. I need to walk off some of this steam and formulate exactly how I want you to help me." She waved a little wave in the air.

CHAPTER SEVEN

*T*he roads had gotten a little more treacherous within the few minutes I was in the theater, but knowing the roads and all the curves down the winding road to my log cabin made it much easier to navigate, since the painted-on lines were completely covered.

Though it normally took me seven minutes to drive to work and just a few more minutes added on to reach downtown, it took me a good twenty minutes until I saw the cute little cabin come into view.

My heart filled with joy when I saw the little puffs of smoke coming from the chimney. Patrick and I loved a good fire in the small potbelly stove, and with the snowy night, it was a perfect setting to snuggle in with the dogs.

The front porch of the cabin happened to be my favorite place and was what really sold me—besides the low price. Aunt Maxi had several rental houses and over the years had accumulated furniture, so I was happy when she gave me the key to her storage unit and let me pick out anything I wanted.

The two rocking chairs my grandfather had made were a perfect addition to the cabin. I changed the pillows on the rockers to match the season, and the Christmas tree pillows I'd recently replaced with the cute snowflake pillows were a perfect match to the weather we were having. And they matched the deep-brown ladder-back-style rockers perfectly.

"Good evening." I walked into the one big room that combined a kitchen and dining room with my hands full of pecan balls and the coffee carafe.

I'd like to say Patrick was quicker than Sassy and Pepper to greet me, but he came in third.

"I'm going to have to jump the couch to beat them," he teased and took the items from my hands so they were free to give the pups some good loving scratches.

"Don't lock the door," I told Patrick after he put the treats on the small table and headed over to the door to lock it. "Aunt Maxi. . ."

"I can't hardly stand it, I'm so mad." Aunt Maxi pushed through the door.

"Is coming over," I muttered under my breath to finish my sentence. I gave Patrick a pinched smile, knowing he was looking forward to a night of the fireplace, the couch, snuggling with the dogs, and mindless television while the snow piled around us.

"Let me help you with your coat." Patrick was such a southern gentleman. He never complained about my mom or Aunt Maxi and their invasive ways when they just barged into our daily lives.

"Thank you. Thank God." Aunt Maxi threw her hands up in the air as if she were in her usual spot in the front row of the Honey Springs Baptist Church. "That Roxanne Bloom came to her senses and moved to Honey Springs and won you back over."

"Won him back over?" I laughed and walked into the kitchen to get the tray of pecan balls and three mugs along with the carafe of coffee.

"It took a lot," Patrick teased, knowing good and well how the story went. When Aunt Maxi turned away to walk into the family room ahead of Patrick, he pointed to her head and mouthed *her hair*.

I had to admit I was a little mean to Patrick when I first moved back. I wasn't in any shape to let a man into my life, but my heart softened as he not only fixed up the coffee shop to code but also changed out all the old tube and knob wiring in the cabin while I had removated it.

With fond memories of how we reconnected the spark we'd started during my summer visits as a teenager and of my practically following him around everywhere, I looked around the cabin and could see how he had his hand in every room of our home.

The bathroom and laundry room were located on the far back right. A set of stairs led up to one big room that was considered the bedroom. The natural light from the skylights and the large window in the bedroom really made the room inviting, but today snow blanketed them, hiding any outside light, though it was really just a grey sky.

That might bother some folks, but I knew that just beyond the clouds was a beautiful sunny sky that would soon make its appearance.

"What's all this business of you being mad?" Patrick and Aunt Maxi headed over to the couches, but not without Pepper pushing himself on Aunt Maxi.

"Roxanne didn't tell you?" She looked between Patrick and me. She only used my full name when she was torn up about something. She was all torn up about this play.

"I just got home," I reminded her and sat down on the couch with my big mug of freshly roasted Columbian.

Pepper jumped up next to me and waited for me to curl up my legs and lay them to my side so he could nestle into their bend. Sassy hung next to Aunt Maxi, who had decided to stand up in front of the fire while she ate a few of the pecan balls.

"Loooow-retta Bebe has decided that our theatrical cast isn't good enough for her time as the head of the committee for the winter theater." Aunt Maxi put her fingertips down for Sassy to lick off the powdered sugar. I snapped my fingers at her, but she ignored me and kept talking. "She has taken my main part and given it to some dried-up actress who owes this director I've never heard of that owed Low-retta a favor." Her eyes narrowed. Her brown eyebrows were hooded like a hawk and did not match her hair at all. "Since when does Low-retta let a favor hang on and not cash it in right away?"

I knew Aunt Maxi was spitfire mad when she continued to

pronounce "Loretta" the way Loretta enunciated her name with her southern accent. She was completely mocking her.

"Then..." Aunt Maxi smacked her hands together, making poor Sassy jump. "The producer tells us tonight that the play the committee had put together, the sweet little romance, has been changed to a murder mystery. One about a young girl who killed her aunt and kept her fur coat, something about a fur coat."

"Gretchen Cannon had on a fur coat. Maybe she is cashing in on her favor to have her play done?" I asked as only a suggestion, but it seemed to make Aunt Maxi's face turn red, and it wasn't because of standing in front of the fire.

"I don't care if Woody Allen himself came to direct this play. It was written by the committee of the Southern Women's Club for the winter theater, and Low-retta or anyone else on the committee *cannot* change it without a vote, and Low-retta didn't do that." Aunt Maxi stomped and made sure she exaggerated her words to get her point across. "And now!" she screamed and jerked some folded-up papers from her pocket before shaking them up in the air. "I only have two pages of script, since I'm nothing more than the maid!"

She took a couple of steps closer to me before she shoved the papers in my face, and she needed to sit down to catch a breath.

"What is this?" I asked and noticed it was really only her part of the play. "Where's the rest of it?"

"That's the crazy part. He said that we don't need the full play and that we will only get the pages when we are on the stage." She shoved a few more pecan balls in her mouth then poured herself a cup of coffee.

She took the time to sip and eat while I read through her lines. It did appear Gretchen had all the lines and Crissy Lane had the lines of the young woman.

"I had no idea Crissy Lane was in it." Reading her name reminded me that I needed to text the group of gals about Emily. "Which reminds me..." I knew I was going to go off subject, and probably the best thing was to get Aunt Maxi stewing on something else. "Emily Rich is closing Bees Knees Bakery and moving out of Honey Springs."

"Moving? Out of Honey Springs?" Aunt Maxi seemed more shocked at this news than what she was mad about. "How could she do that? What about her parents? I just saw Evan down at the bank today, and he didn't mention a word of it."

"I don't know anything about that, but it's a done deal. She's sold all the bakery equipment and even has a moving date for next week." A deep, sorrowful sigh escaped me before I took another drink of coffee.

"This is great coffee, by the way." Patrick's arm was lying across the back of the couch and was long enough for his fingertips to scratch at my back. "New roast?"

"Mmm-hmmm, the Honduras bag." I couldn't help but well up with pride because he was right. It was a nice, full-bodied, rich coffee that I knew was going to sell well when I debuted it for the spring collection. "Which I was roasting when Emily came in to see me before I left for home. She actually said something that made me think."

"Uh-oh." Patrick smiled. "When you start thinking about something, I know something is going to happen."

"She mentioned something about me taking over the bakery space for a roastery." Saying it out loud actually gave me a little tickle in my belly which told me there was a little something to it. "She even suggested having roastery tours and maybe some roasting classes."

"I can see by the fire in your eyes that you're thinking on it." Aunt Maxi smiled. "So maybe her leaving isn't a bad idea. I could use the distraction."

"What?" Patrick and I both said in unison for her to clarify.

"You're going to need someone to run it. I am the perfect person." She shrugged and popped another pecan ball in her mouth.

"First off, you're going to get sick." I uncurled my feet, causing Pepper to jump up, and leaned over to grab the tray before I got up and took the sweet treats into the kitchen. "Secondly, you don't even know how to use the roaster I have now."

"I might be old, but this old dog does learn new tricks." She straightened her shoulders back and lifted her chin in the air. "I don't need you to pay me."

"It's not that, Maxine." Patrick also took the liberty to chime in. "But you're retired. Enjoying your life. Why would you want to spend your days roasting coffee?"

Though I knew Patrick was trying to sway her as I wanted him to, what he said really got my attention.

"So...." I hesitated and stopped in front of the couch where he was sitting. "You think it's a good idea and I should buy the building even though it's not next to the Bean Hive?"

"I think that Queen for the Day is looking to expand. Even though the Bees Knees isn't as wide on the inside as Queen for the Day, it's got more square footage in length and exactly what Tamara McFee is looking for." Patrick would know, since he was the contractor most businesses used. "She was seriously considering moving off the board-walk to find a bigger space, but this might work out perfectly."

"Then I could take her shop, which is right next door." The idea was coming together.

"If the city council agrees." Aunt Maxi just had to throw a wrench in it. "But I know people." She gave me a wink.

"If I give you a job?" I asked, knowing her wink came with a catch.

"Mmmhhhh," she ho-hummed with a big smile across her face and then took another drink of her coffee.

CHAPTER EIGHT

The alarm went off so fast that I didn't even feel like I'd gone to sleep. Last night, after Aunt Maxi seemed to calm down about her small part in the play, we talked about the possibilities of what a roaster could do for Honey Springs.

While the men went on their fishing trips, we could offer a roasting class for the women along with some cool facials and spa treatments using coffee if I could get the Honey Comb Salon to agree. They were a few doors down, and we could make it a package. I'd even go as far as putting something together for All About the Details and the bridal events they hosted. Bridal parties were always coming into the Bean Hive to grab coffee while they were waiting for the appointment with Babette Cliff, the owner.

Honey Springs was a destination for all things romantic. Most of the tourists rented cabins for honeymoons, girls' weekends, family trips, and other gatherings. Maybe a roastery would just add to the experiences our small southern town offered.

Still, it was definitely something for me to consider, and I would ask Crissy Lane when I texted her about Emily. Aunt Maxi always told me God made everything happen for a reason, and though I hated to see

Emily move away from Honey Springs, I couldn't help but think Aunt Maxi's way of looking at things just might be right in this case.

Like always, Pepper and I got up out of the comfy white iron bed suite that I'd also gotten from Aunt Maxi's storage unit when I moved in. I tiptoed down to the bathroom to get ready.

This was the reason I kept my work clothes in the laundry room. I didn't want to have to wake Patrick since my wake-up time was around four-thirty a.m. and his was around six.

Sassy wasn't about to budge and Pepper curled up in his little bed in front of the potbelly stove that still glowed red through the small window on the door.

After I took a few minutes to get ready and throw another log on the fire so Patrick and Sassy would have a warm house to wake up to, Pepper and I were out the door.

"It looks like the road crew really worked hard last night." I talked to Pepper, who was busy standing up on the arm of the door and looking out the window as if he could really see something through the darkness.

The sun wouldn't pop up until around seven a.m., and the sunrise would only start to get earlier, since we were headed into spring. The long, dark, and really cold mornings were almost behind us, and a new life would soon bring Honey Springs alive with fresh Kentucky bluegrass, daffodils, lilacs, and spring mix that painted the season of spring.

It only took us seven minutes to pull into the boardwalk parking lot. There weren't any lights on in any of the stores on the boardwalk when we passed, which was normal for our usual start time. But I knew to expect a lot of the owners to start trickling into their shops in about an hour, stopping at the Bean Hive to get their morning caffeine fix.

"What do you think about a roastery?" I asked Pepper and stopped in front of the Queen for the Day clothing boutique. "I can totally picture a small roaster in the display window to pull in customers."

Pepper danced around my feet, and I took it as a sign that he totally agreed with me.

"Pepper..." I looked down at my sweet Schnauzer and into his big round black eyes. "I think we are in trouble. I've already got the roastery details in my head, and when I get something in my head…."

He darted off to the front door of the Bean Hive, and I followed him. Then I unlocked the door.

"Good morning, Mocha," I called out and ran my hand up the wall to flip on the interior lights of the coffee shop.

Pepper had already darted inside. Light or not, he never waited.

I was happy to see Mocha was curled up in the dog bed in front of the fireplace. She didn't run off when Pepper hurried over to greet her. She simply stretched out her arms and gave a great big yawn.

"We need to get this fire going." I noticed it was a tad bit chilly. I peeled off my coat and laid it across the arm of the couch. I started to stack up kindling and some newspapers before I threw the match in the wood fireplace to get a nice bed of coals going there.

After Pepper greeted Mocha, he left her alone and sat in front of his bowl.

"I know, you're hungry." I grabbed my coat, and when I passed Pepper and his empty bowl, I reached down and scratched the top of his head before I hung my coat up on the coat rack. I retrieved a scoop of his food. "Here you go."

He chowed down, and I walked along the industrial coffee pots behind the counter, flipping them to brew. Then I headed back into the kitchen, where I turned on the three ovens for preheating and flipped on my little coffee pot filled with the new Columbian coffee I'd just roasted yesterday.

The sausage casserole was pretty much a staple around here for customers during the winter months. It was a comfort to the soul, and all the cheese made it perfect. We southerners loved a good comfort food.

I retrieved a couple of the glass casserole dishes from the walk-in freezer and took them over to the oven, where I set them on top of the stove while I waited for the ovens to preheat.

"Hey, you two," I said, greeting Pepper and Mocha when they came into the kitchen together. "I see you've made friends."

Though it made me happy to see Mocha making friends with Pepper, I really needed her to make friends with customers so we could get her into her forever home.

"I need to text Crissy and the girls." It might seem odd to some people that I talked to the animals like they were human, but they made me feel happy and kept me company. There was nothing like a great conversation with an animal because no matter how wrong or misguided, as we like to say in the south, about how we might feel about something, the animals always appeared to agree with me.

Hey girls! I'm sure y'all are as sad as I am about Emily moving, but we all want what is best for her. I would like to invite everyone to the coffee shop so we can discuss how we can send off our dear friend with a see-you-soon party because we know this isn't goodbye. Please let me know if late afternoon today works to meet. We don't have a lot of time to plan. Xoxoxo Roxy.

"There. That should do it." I put my phone down just as someone was knocking on the door. "It's a bit early for Bunny, and I don't have to pick up the pecan ring from Emily for a couple of hours," I told Pepper and Mocha on my way to see who was at the door.

The pitter-patter of their feet made me smile, telling me they were following me to the door. If it weren't for the sweeping lashes and great big smile, I'd have mistaken the blond-haired woman for Aunt Maxi, but Crissy Lane was standing at the door in all her glory, waving, when she noticed me walking to let her in.

"Hi do, Roxy." Crissy walked through the door, wearing a bright-blue fluffy coat. She gave me a hug, and though the coat looked like something my grandmother would have covering the lid of her toilet, it was soft to the touch. "I just got your text on the way to the salon, so I figured I'd just stop right on in and grab my coffee early so we can discuss."

"Good morning." I laughed at Crissy's typical behavior.

We southerners liked to just drop in. We didn't bother calling or texting when we were about to stop over. If the desire to pop in washed over us, we just did it, and we weren't expected to call either.

"I'm glad you're here." I locked the door back after she came on in. "That's Mocha, the Pet Palace animal of the week. Isn't she a doll?"

Crissy was like me. She loved all animals.

"How about a cup of coffee while we talk?" I loved seeing her bright smiling face in the morning.

"Yes. It's so cold out there. I can't believe the snow was so heavy it snapped the internet lines." The red freckles on her face widened as she frowned, which was how you knew she was a natural redhead. Her false eyelashes swooped down her cheeks, drawing a shadow along her cheeks.

"The internet is down?" I questioned and headed right on over to the register, where we used the Square application on the iPad.

"Yeah. Of course, I tried to get on social media first thing, and when I couldn't connect, I nearly had a heart attack. I flipped on the radio and heard the weather report about how the snow was so heavy on the lines that some power is out and the internet is out." While she told me her whole morning routine and how this was going to affect her day, I tapped and poked the iPad alive, only to find out she was right.

I would still be able to take orders and process credit cards through the Square. The payments were just going to have to be offline. They would quickly recover automatically once the internet came back.

"I hope it comes back on before we open." I glanced up at the clock and realized that was in only an hour.

"The radio report said it could be days in some areas." Crissy made herself at home, which was expected. She waved her phone in the air. Her dime-store square solitaire diamond flashed as she wiggled it around.

Like Patrick and I, Crissy and I had formed a relationship when I was visiting Aunt Maxi on all those summer vacations. Crissy was loud, boisterous, and fun, making it easy for her to make friends and enjoyable to be around.

When I moved to Honey Springs, she'd gotten me into a community of girlfriends that made my transition to living here very easy.

"I'm going to have to show Bunny how to process a sale without the internet." Not that it was too difficult, but Bunny was up there in years, and I tried to make working, or, as she put it, *getting out of the house*, easy for her.

"I can be here later today. I've got to run through rehearsal then color Mae Belle Donovan's hair." She made herself a big cup of coffee in a mug, which told me she would hang out for a minute.

"I heard you were in the big production that seems to be causing a lot of controversy." It was my chance to poke around, and Crissy was the perfect person to do it with because she loved to talk, so she had the perfect job.

"Let me tell you how it happened."

She moved around to the stool on the side of the counter while I headed over to stoke the fire. Then I started to refill the coffee-and-tea station, since I didn't do it last night before I left.

"I was already in the play Loretta had written." She rolled her eyes and took a sip of coffee.

"Keep talking," I called to her over my shoulder on the way back to the kitchen. "I've got to get the casseroles in the oven."

"Loretta was in my chair, getting her hair dyed, which we all know is from the bottle, though she'd as soon die as admit to it." Crissy always told it like it was, and I admired that about her.

She talked about Loretta for a few more minutes, giving me the opportunity to get the casseroles in the oven and a few of the other frozen pastries out of the freezer. I dumped some of the pecan balls I'd made last night on a serving platter. Then I reached under the preparation island to grab one of the mini chalkboards to place beside the platter in the glass display case.

"She told me she needed a scene in her play where the heroine is getting her hair done for the ending of the wedding. She wanted it to be real with real language and all, so of course she came to me." She shrugged, bringing her shoulders up to her ears. "I'm always about helping people out."

I grabbed the piece of chalk next to the register and quickly wrote the name of the pastry on the small chalkboard then put it in the glass case.

She gave me a theatrical wink. You know, the long and slow type with her lip hiked up really high to one side?

"Yeah. You're for sure that." I patted her shoulder on my way across the coffee shop to the coffee bar. I opened the bar stand cabinet and took out the contents that needed refilling—the small packs of differently flavored coffee creamers, the various sugar packets and non-sugar packets, coffee stirrers, and a few lids, just to name a few. "Who do you think you're talking to? You can't pull the wool over my eyes," I teased and went behind the counter to retrieve the free-standing coffee carafes just in time for the kitchen timer to ding.

"Just as luck would have it," she continued when I went into the kitchen to retrieve the casserole and put more casseroles in the oven to heat through since I'd already pre-cooked them. "Alan loved my small performance, and when he changed the play, he said I was perfect as the murderer."

"Murderer?" My head shot up when I put the casserole dish on the counter and took off the oven gloves. I left the casserole dish there to cool so I could cut really nice thick slices.

"Yeah." Crissy and I both looked back at the door when it dinged at Bunny's arrival. "It's an awesome story."

"Good morning," I said to Bunny and helped her with her coat. "You're a little early."

"I wanted to make sure I gave myself plenty of time if the roads were bad, but they weren't." She took the bobby pins that had spilled out of her pillbox hat from her hair and started her routine of putting her coat, hat, and pocketbook away while she grabbed an apron. "What's going on with you today, Crissy?"

"Oh the usual, being a star and stuff." Crissy loved to pique everyone's interest about what she had going on. "I was just telling Roxy how Alan Bogart loved my acting skills and moved me to the second lead in the new murder mystery play."

"Is that right?" Bunny asked and kept hitting the keys on the iPad so she could sign into her time card.

"Internet is down," I whispered on my way back into the kitchen so as not to disrupt Crissy's story because she kept on talking. Didn't miss a beat.

"It's really good. There is an old lady, played by Gretchen, of course, who is a grandmother to this killer, *moi*." She had her hand on her chest when I walked back into the coffee shop with the other casserole.

Bunny had already taken the liberty of cutting the cooling casserole and putting the slices in the brown wrapping made specifically to keep the items warm. Then she set them on a tiered tray in the glass counter where I'd placed the mini chalkboard.

"The granddaughter kills the grandmother. It's fabulous. Like no other murder mystery you've ever seen." Crissy stood up and walked over to the coffee bar, where she retrieved a to-go cup.

"How do you know all the plot?" I questioned. "Aunt Maxi only got two sheets of her role. She said Alan didn't want people to worry about the other roles or something like that."

"Yes," she said with a gasp. "I'm the only one with the full manuscript," she squealed. "But I must go. The stage calls."

"Which reminds me that I need to get my coffee over there before the big seven a.m. curtain call." I shook my head and waved to Crissy.

"I'll see you there, and I'll be back this afternoon for the see-you-later party planning." She waved goodbye to Bunny and me before she disappeared into the dark morning.

"See-you-later planning?" Bunny asked and walked over to the fire-place with a salmon treat each for Mocha and Pepper.

Pepper didn't care whether it was a cat treat or dog treat. He just liked treats.

"I have unfortunate news about Emily Rich." I headed over to the shop door and flipped the Closed sign on the door to the Open side. "She's closing Bees Knees and moving out of town. So the gals and I are going to throw her a see-you-later get-together instead of a goodbye party."

"I never thought of anyone leaving Honey Springs." Bunny loved our little small town so much. She was a staple of our community and a very good person... when Aunt Maxi wasn't around.

"I know I'm not going anywhere." I untied my apron from around my waist and took my coat off the coat rack. "Do you mind putting a couple more carafes on? I've got to get these down to the theater and come back to take those to the Cocoon."

I did a few clicks of my tongue to get Pepper's attention so he knew we were heading out the door. Plus it was a great time for him to go potty.

"No problem. Be careful out there," Bunny called on my way out the door. "And I don't mean the weather. I mean all the big heads at the theater."

I giggled, knowing exactly how right Bunny was about the divas all in one room. Unfortunately, a tickle in my gut told me to hold on because we were in for a big production, and I was not sure it would be worthy of a five-star review.

CHAPTER NINE

"You be on your best behavior," I told Pepper after we walked into the theater. "Not that I don't expect you to behave, but there's a lot of people in there."

My hands were filled by the pecan ring Emily had given me on my way here and the carafe of coffee. While I tried to focus on getting Gretchen's request into her room, my mind continued to wander because of the question Emily posed when I picked up the pastry. She'd asked me if I'd thought about the idea of turning the bakery into a roastery.

I did tell her that the idea interested me, but there was a big issue that stood in the way... the other two buildings.

There was really no time to worry about that right now. What was important in this moment was getting the pastries in Gretchen's dressing room before she noticed they weren't there.

All the lights were on inside the theater, and people were milling around. Most of them I knew I liked and some of them I didn't.

"Good morning, Bev," I said to Bev Teagarden when she passed me with a big flower arrangement I'd seen on display in the Wild and Whimsy.

"Hiya, Roxy." She shuffled past, making sure she didn't whack me with the arrangement. "This whole change of plans has really thrown a wrench in our day. I'm not sure if this producer knows exactly what he's doing."

I smiled, trying not to gossip about my thoughts on Alan and how he had handled the switch over of props and actors for the new play he'd implemented. Then I headed straight to the craft table, where I set up the table of goodies for the crew of the production. Next, I headed off to Gretchen Cannon's dressing room with her own personal treats, which Sydney had requested.

"Knock, knock," I said to announce my entrance when I pushed open the door to Gretchen's dressing room with my toe, happy to see the door was cracked. "Good. Not here yet."

The lights in the dressing room were off, but the lights from the hallway added a nice glow to the room. That way, I could see the exact spot I'd scoped out the night before to put her pecan ring and coffee.

I'd put a few napkins with the Bean Hive logo in my bag to go along with the display in Gretchen's room to make it a little more presentable. Emily had put the pecan ring on a plastic decorative tray Gretchen could throw away when she was finished.

"Not here yet?" Mark Redding stood at the dressing room door, catching me off guard. "Sorry if I scared you."

"I'm good. I wasn't expecting anyone. I was focused on getting this set up just right before Gretchen gets here." I smiled and added the finishing touches to improve the presentation.

"Southern women sure do like everyone to feel at home." Mark Redding walked in and fiddled with the briefcase.

It was the same briefcase I had seen Alan digging through, and I wondered why he left it in there. The thought quickly slipped my mind when I heard voices.

"I'm getting out of here before I have to interact with anyone." I grabbed my bag from the floor and met Mark out in the hallway, where he was busy patting Pepper. "So, let me guess, Camey Montgomery is going out of her way to make everyone welcome."

The voices were coming from the front of the theater down the left, so I took a right with Mark following next to me.

"She's amazing. I've never stayed at a hotel so welcoming." He twisted to the side when we passed someone so he didn't bump into them. The glare the man gave Mark didn't go unnoticed. "This is turning out to be a big deal. I see Alan's production crew is here."

"So that's where all these people came from," I said since I'd noticed a lot of faces that I didn't recognize hurrying around. "Let me guess, they all can't stand you."

"Only because of him." Mark's head tilted to the stage when we walked into the side door of the theater.

For a couple of seconds, we watched Alan Bogart as he directed people to go here and there. What I figured was the manuscript was folded in half under his arm.

"Go down! Down! I said go down!" Alan screamed at the top of his lungs with a vicious tone and pointed at the lights.

As he yelled some more, the lighting guy was tilting, twisting, and rotating until Alan had agreed it wasn't perfect but would do.

"See, he just can't give compliments or be nice. I swear after he had that heart attack and needed a blood transfusion, they gave him blood from the devil himself." Mark's words made me giggle. "It's true. The reviewers thought his life-changing surgery would make him a little more compassionate, but it made him worse."

"That's a shame." My eyes swept up to the entrance, where the center aisle started, and I noticed Gretchen and Sydney were standing there. "They're here."

"And everyone else better get here or Gretchen and Alan will have what you guys around here call a hissy fit." He pointed at the front row, and I followed him there. "Might as well have a front-row seat to the show."

We slipped into the seats with no one even noticing. The crew was busy making the adjustments to some of the props Bev Teagarden had brought, and another crew member helped take out some of the props that were supposed to go with the original script by Loretta Bebe.

"Okay, everyone!" Alan clapped his hands. "It's time for the morning meeting per your schedule. Time is money, and money is time."

"Schedule?" I whispered to Mark.

"Oh yeah, he keeps a pretty tight schedule to keep everyone moving. That's one of the reasons so many actors won't work for him. If they are even one second late, he fires them." Mark's brows rose. "Back in the day, his heyday, it worked. Not too many agents or lawyers involved. But up there."

I followed Mark's eyes as they shifted up to the balcony.

"Those are lawyers and agents." He'd pointed out the group of about ten people gathered in the balcony with their heads buried in their phones. "The actors claim all sorts of things if things don't go their way."

"I have to say that I'm glad I'm no longer a practicing lawyer." I smiled.

"Get out. You?" Mark drew back. His brows furrowed. "Sweet and southern you were a lawyer?"

"I'm still a lawyer, just not practicing full time."

The lights went down, and we shifted forward to watch the stage.

"This is not going to do!" Gretchen hurried onto the stage. Sydney had stopped shy of the steps going up to the stage. "I have three pages of lines, and I want the entire manuscript."

"Here we go." Mark leaned over and continued, "Gretchen has been a pain all morning. Starting with the hotel. I could hear her clear up to my room, fussing with someone in the lobby. I couldn't make it out, but I think it was Alan. It was a man's voice."

"Really?" I asked and made a mental note to ask Camey all about it... over a cup of coffee, of course.

"Thanks for the coffee." Loretta Bebe had snuck in behind us and leaned on the back of my chair. "This has been a nightmare. I'm a little upset I called in my favor now."

I reached around with my hand and patted her arm. Loretta had to be upset if she was thanking me for the coffee. Normally, she'd just go on about her business.

"We had a sweet love story, and now he's doing murder. I'm beside myself over it, and I've got to get all the committee to up my budget so I can change the marketing materials. I had hearts on everything. Now I guess I've got to put knives or some sort of dripping blood." She shivered. "The thought makes me so upset. What will the church group think?"

"You're the one who didn't question him." Alan shrugged.

Uh-oh, I thought when Loretta jerked back, glaring at Alan. She stood up, tugged on the edges of her pink suit coat, and straightened herself to look presentable before she marched off.

"What was that?" he asked while we both watched her march up the steps and engage in the meeting Alan was having with the actors, including Crissy and Aunt Maxi.

"You've just gotten on Low-retta Bebe's bad side." I laughed.

"I seem to do that to a lot of people." He nodded toward the stage then took out his camera. "Here we go. The real show is about to start."

"I told you that I'm not going to play some old lady!" Gretchen's hands fisted. "You told me I'd be playing a young, vivacious actor."

"That was before I got my hands on the new script." Alan jerked the papers from his armpit and shook them in the air. "That was before the mystery."

"That wasn't the favor I called in on, Alan Bogart, and you know it." Gretchen's lips were moving a mile a minute, and the spit flowed out from her mouth like a sprinkler.

Sydney practically tiptoed onto the stage and around the group, making her way over to Gretchen.

"Stop this nonsense right now!" Alan pointed directly at Gretchen. "If it weren't for me, you'd not be here." Then he looked directly at Loretta and pointed. "If it weren't for me, this little romance production you had going would have brought this theater under!" Alan held his hand up over his eyes and looked out into the crowd. When he caught sight of Mark Redding, he pointed at him. "I told you never to show up to anything I'm doing! Get out of here, or I'll make sure you don't have a job at the *Times* when you get back to New York!"

Alan sucked in a big deep breath before turning around to face all the actors.

"I want five minutes to myself. In that five minutes…" He held up his hand. He had stubby fingers. "If you do not want to be a member of this cast and crew, I suggest you clear your things and leave. There are plenty of people around here that I can make a star! And younger."

The last jab had to be for Gretchen because he looked directly at her.

"You'll regret this." She stomped off the stage with Sydney in tow.

"I'm guessing this is my time to leave or at least hide." Mark excused himself.

The only people left on stage were Aunt Maxi and Crissy. Both had shocked looks on their faces.

"You stay," I told Pepper, who was lying underneath the theater chair. "If you were to go up there and scratch the floor, Alan would have you banned."

Pepper's ears perked up.

"You're a good boy." I made my way to the steps and over to Aunt Maxi and Crissy. "That was harsh."

"I agree about him changing the script." Aunt Maxi harrumphed, crossing her arms.

"I'm the opposite. I've been practicing my lines all night." Crissy held up the thick manuscript.

Aunt Maxi's jaw dropped.

"Is that the full play?" she asked Crissy.

"Mmm-hhhhm. I've got the biggest part, and I'm the killer." Crissy took real pride in claiming that.

"There's one thing for sure. Low-retta is not happy." I couldn't help but look over where she'd disappeared, but everyone was gone. Everyone but Alan Bogart, who was looking at his watch.

"Here he comes." Crissy stiffened and shifted toward the little circle the three of us had formed.

"I see we have two actors who'd like to get instructions from me."

Alan's chin lifted. "There's something to say about you two ladies and the pride you take in your craft."

"I'm beyond thrilled to be playing a killer," Crissy started to say, but the ropes dangling behind us flew up in the air, smacking the velvet curtain behind them.

"Watch out!" I yelled and pushed Aunt Maxi out of the way when I noticed the ropes were attached to the sandbags overhead that kept the equipment in place.

Aunt Maxi and I fell to the ground just in time. She looked at me with wide eyes.

"Are you okay?" I asked her and used my hands to push myself up on my knees to help her up. I glanced above my head when I heard some footsteps.

Was someone up there?

My eyes narrowed to see through the dark for any shadows. A sliver of light peeked through what appeared to be a door opening then closing quickly.

"Yeah. I'm fine. I think." Aunt Maxi brought my attention back to her. She patted around her body and then took my outstretched hand to help her up.

"I'm not!" Crissy yelled.

I looked up and across Alan's body to find one of the sandbags had landed on Crissy's leg.

"I think my leg is broken." She winced in pain as Aunt Maxi walked closer to her.

"I think he's dead." Aunt Maxi stood over Alan Bogart's body.

CHAPTER TEN

*I*t didn't take long for Spencer Shepard of the Honey Springs sheriff's department to show up and not too long after that for Crissy Lane to pour on the tears so Spencer could console her.

Granted, Spencer was single and very handsome in his sheriff's uniform, and his sandy hair and piercing green eyes weren't bad either.

"I don't know what happened," Crissy whined to Spencer's question he'd had for her about the time of the incident. She was still sitting on the floor with her hand on her leg while the EMT put a brace on it. She whimpered as they hoisted her onto a stretcher that was waiting for her off stage where the audience would sit. "One minute we were discussing my leading role, and the next minute I heard the cord of the sandbag zipping up the curtain, and before I knew it, I was knocked on the ground. When I looked up, Roxy and Maxine were over there, and Alan was between us." Crissy batted her eyes at Spencer.

I wasn't sure whether or not he noticed her flirting between the whines and whimpers, but he sure didn't lead on. He kept his eyes on the notebook in which he wrote down what she'd been saying.

"Spencer, can I talk to you privately?" I asked when I noticed Gretchen Cannon, Sydney O'Neil, Loretta Bebe, and Mark Redding were standing stage right in a huddle with their heads together.

Every once in a while, Loretta popped her head out and chin up over the heads of the others to see if she could hear what was going on. In true Loretta fashion, she reported back what she could hear. Trust me. I knew her gig because I'd been in various situations in Loretta's little huddle.

"Sure." Spencer nodded. "Can you please get Crissy on over to the hospital to get her leg checked out?" he told more than asked the EMT. "Does anyone else need to see the EMT before they head on out?" Spencer asked the crowd but looked at Aunt Maxi since I had pushed her out of the way, making her fall.

When no one, not even Aunt Maxi, stepped up, he gave the go-ahead for them to take Crissy.

"I'll call you when I leave here," I assured her and walked her out of the theater so she wasn't alone. Pepper trotted next to me.

"I might need you to bring me some magazines if the internet doesn't come back up soon." She waved her phone in the air.

Her leg must not have been hurting her too badly if she was worried about her social media.

When the EMTs got her into the ambulance, she gave the most pitiful wave before they shut the door. Pepper and I stood there watching the ambulance drive off.

"You can sit in the car for a few minutes," I told Pepper and put him in the car, where he immediately snuggled up on his blanket in the passenger seat. "And you have water too."

I took out the dog bag I kept in the door's storage holder. I put his water bowl on the floorboard and filled it halfway with the bottled water and set a few treats next to it.

When I walked back into the theater, I noticed Spencer had walked over to Kevin Roberts, the coroner. They whispered a few words before Kevin pointed to Spencer's neck. He handed Spencer a clipboard. Spencer signed something, which I assumed was the paperwork needed for Kevin to remove Alan's body because Kevin had already gotten Alan on the gurney. He tugged it up and rolled him down the ramp with the clipboard on top of Alan's body.

"What was it that you needed?" Spencer walked over to Aunt Maxi and me. "Hello." He waved his hands in front of me.

"Sorry. I was just looking at Kevin." I gnawed my lip. "You know, I don't know him that well. The only time I see him is when there's been a murder, and I'm not so sure this was an accident."

The only reasons I used the word "accident" were that I'd overheard the others answering Spencer's questions by saying what a terrible accident this was and that Spencer had even referred to it as an accident.

"Roxy," he said in an exhausted tone. "You and I both know this old theater is so rickety and outdated. It's used four times a year, and ropes start to deteriorate."

"I agree, but when I was helping Aunt Maxi up after I'd pushed her out of the way, I heard footsteps up there." I glanced up. "Shortly after I heard them, I saw a sliver of light shine through an open door before it closed."

Spencer moved his face towards Aunt Maxi but kept his eyes on me for a few seconds before he finally asked Aunt Maxi, "Did you see or hear anything?"

"Not a darn thing. All I know was one minute I was about to complain about my two little pages of script, and the next I was thanking the good Lord above for sparing me the knock on the head. Now that I see it took out Alan, I'm very grateful for the shove." She nodded at me with big eyes.

"Are you absolutely sure you heard footsteps?" He shifted back to me. "I mean, you were under a lot of stress in that moment."

"Yes, Spencer. I heard footsteps and saw a door open. I know what I saw." There was no mistaking what I'd seen, and I had a hard time believing the cords had simply deteriorated and no one had noticed.

"You didn't see who it was?" he asked, and I slowly shook my head. "Man? Woman?"

"Nope. Just footsteps. But give me a few hours, and I'll see if I can remember anything else." It was a technique I used to use with my clients when I was a lawyer.

If they called me after a traumatic experience and they had to be questioned by the police, I suggested the police wait to interview them because the client was so shocked or ridden with anxiety they weren't thinking as clearly as they could. Generally, it would be days or even weeks after their mind relaxed that they would recall small details that helped paint the bigger picture. I was no different.

Though I didn't believe I was in shock, I could've been, and I could've blocked any sort of details to tell whether this was an accident or homicide.

"Plus there aren't a lack of suspects that would love to see Alan Bogart in the state he's in now." The words accidentally left my mouth, and I threw my hand over it.

"All right." Spencer's eyes narrowed suspiciously. "What is going on in that head of yours?"

"Nothing," I lied. "What did Kevin say?"

"At initial glance, it appears as if the sandbag hit him perfectly on top of his head, breaking his neck and causing instant death. Probably didn't see it coming." Spencer frowned.

"Spencer." Loretta stalked over, and her little gossip group had all turned to watch her. "Just when do you think this little fiasco will be cleaned up? We have a play to rehearse." She clasped her hands together in front of her. "The play must go on."

"Alan would've wanted that," Gretchen said and dabbed the edges of her eyes, adding a little sniffle.

Mark Redding wasn't about to let this moment pass without taking photos and getting comments from the various actors and crew members.

"I think you're done for today. We need a little time to process the scene," he told Loretta with a follow-up glance to the group.

"Process the scene?" Loretta asked nervously. "That's normally not done unless you think there was foul play."

The group of actors and crew members walked over in full earshot of what Spencer had to say.

"Let's just say I'm not ruling this out as a homicide. We'd like to make sure there isn't any evidence of that, and it'll give us time to process your statements and where each one of you were during the time of the incident."

Spencer might've had their attention when he addressed them, but the one word that had caught my attention was that he'd changed from his previous statement of "accident" to "incident." Two very different scenes in the investigation world.

"Who on earth would want to harm Alan?" Gretchen asked and looked around.

"Oh, come off it." Aunt Maxi pointed a finger at Gretchen. "By the way I hear tell, you had the biggest beef with him about your role in this play, and he owed you a favor. Some favor payback for him to switch your role at the last minute, and if you're all worried about your career, becoming the B-class actress he insinuated you're becoming is humiliating."

"I mean, Maxine might have a point." Loretta chimed in like she was trying to take the heat off her. "You did just ask me to put you back in the lead role."

"I cannot believe my ears." Gretchen's mouth dropped. She looked to Sydney to save her.

"Those are ridiculous accusations. Miss Cannon has nothing but love and respect for a producer as amazing as Alan Bogart." Sydney took Gretchen by the shoulders. "I honestly can't believe you."

"Me?" Loretta pointed at herself.

"Yes, you." Sydney was direct. "You just asked Gretchen for more help on the production, and now you go pointing fingers at her as if she killed someone when she isn't obligated to stay here, since she no longer has to fulfill the favor to Alan now that he's dead."

"Another motive to have killed the man," Aunt Maxi muttered, elbowing me in the ribs.

"I just can't help direct." Gretchen brought the hanky back up to her eyes and dabbed them again. "I just can't do it all."

I watched Spencer's amused reaction while the group of actors turned on one another.

"But you said you'd help me." Loretta had already moved on from pointing out Gretchen's flaws with her fingers and practically began to beg for her help.

"I can't take this stress. You claim I killed my friend when you have the best motive to have killed him." Gretchen's tears dried up awfully fast. "He owed you a favor, and when he switched the play from the two-bit romance you wrote to this genius murder mystery, your head spun around five times on your shoulders. You have a reputation to uphold in this community, and if you think for one second that I believe that you don't lie in a tanning bed, you're crazy!"

Loretta went from a southern lady to a hot mess within half a second.

"Now, now, ladies." Sydney stepped between the two feuding women. "Tearing each other down isn't going to get us any closer to production. Let's let Mr. Shephard do his job and we collect our thoughts. If we need a production manager, I'm more than happy to step up to the plate."

"She does have her degree in film." Gretchen nodded.

"Agree to regroup tomorrow?" Sydney looked at everyone for confirmation. Everyone nodded. "Great. I have the text thread from Alan, so we will continue to communicate through that."

After it was all said and done, Spencer was busy looking around, and everyone else had gone their separate ways. Everyone but Aunt Maxi, Loretta, and me.

"That woman," Loretta spat, referring to Gretchen Cannon. "She's so sorry I wouldn't wave at her if my arm was on fire."

"Don't you pay her any mind, Low-retta." Aunt Maxi took her by the arm and guided her out of the theater. "Our town will love our play no matter who is in it or who produces it."

"Not if we have a murder on our hands." Loretta looked at me with the most pitiful downturned eyes. "Do you think they think I'm a suspect?"

"Don't you worry yourself about that until Spencer comes back with Kevin's report." I tried to make Loretta feel better, but I'd been around this block a time or two.

I knew what I heard and what I saw, and I was pretty positive Spencer's report would come back as an official homicide.

CHAPTER ELEVEN

"*W*hat on earth is going on over at the theater?" Bunny Bowowski couldn't hightail it over fast enough to me when she saw Pepper and me come through the coffee shop door.

That there were so many customers shouldn't've surprised me because whenever there was a situation in Honey Springs, including simple gossip, they loved to come to the coffee shop to have a cup of coffee and hear the rumor mill.

I'd like to say it was awful that they did this, but it was good for business.

"You aren't going to believe it," I muttered under my breath and took a look into Mocha's cage on my way back to the counter. Bunny followed on my heels.

"Roxy!"

I was slipping off my coat and on my way back to the counter to hang it up when I heard someone calling my name.

"Roxy!"

"It's that reporter." Bunny snarled and put her hands on me to guide me back to the counter as though she were protecting me. "He's trying to get the scoop."

"The scoop? He was there." I hung my coat up and waved him over to me. "He might have some good information for us."

"For us?" Bunny jerked back. "Oh no. Don't you dare tell me you're going to stick your nose into this." She waited for me to respond. When I didn't, she threw her arms up in the air. "Of course you are going to. Why wouldn't you? You think that producer was murdered, don't you?"

"Bunny, Mark and I are going to go into the kitchen." I scanned the glass display case to see what I needed to thaw and replace while I was back there. "I'll grab some more donuts, blueberry scones, and some maple glazed long johns."

"And that blend you had."

"Blend?" Frantically, I turned around and looked at the small container I'd roasted from the very expensive Honduras burlap bag.

"Yeah. That stuff sold out fast." She shrugged and waddled back over to the register when someone came up to pay. "I want to know every single detail of what happened after I get some of these people out of here."

Mark followed me through the push-through door into the kitchen.

"You can sit there." I pointed to the stool butted up to the work-station.

While he got situated, I headed straight to the freezer and grabbed the few items to thaw and restock.

"That should keep us until lunch." I was mainly talking to myself like I always did, but Mark nodded in agreement. "And while those thaw..." I continued and tugged the big dry-erase whiteboard from underneath the workstation, laid it on top, and grabbed the dry-erase marker from the drawer. "We can talk about who had the most motive."

"Whoa!" Mark eased up onto his feet. His jaw dropped when he noticed I'd written Alan Bogart's name at the top and the word Victim under it. "What are you doing?"

"Obviously one of the crew or the actors killed Alan." I quickly wrote down Gretchen's name. "But who?" I wiggled the marker toward him. "I saw you talking to the crew, and I don't know them, but I'd love to read your notes."

"Wait." Mark's mouth opened, closed, and opened before his head tilted to the left, and he pursed his lips. "Are you saying Alan was murdered?"

"Well, yeah." I noticed his state of befuddlement. "Don't you?"

"I never thought..." He hesitated. "But the officer guy said the theater was old and the rope was probably deteriorated."

"Deteriorated my patootie!" Low-retta swept through the door with Aunt Maxi on her heels. "The theater has an inspection once a year in January. And it passed with flying colors. Nothing about the ropes and nothing about the sandbags."

"I did hear something from the catwalk right before the bags came down, and I saw the door up there open and close right after the bags fell," I told them. "I told Spencer too."

My words met with a collective gasp.

"Think about it. Gretchen Cannon was here for a favor. It was no secret she wasn't happy he changed the script. What was the favor?" I tapped the marker on the whiteboard as I tried to collect my thoughts. "Then you and Alan sure did have a volatile relationship." I pointed at Mark and then wondered if he should be here.

"Me? I was sitting with you the entire time. I don't know my way around the theater." He scowled at me. "Besides, we don't even know if he was murdered."

"You know what?" I grabbed the hand towel sitting on the workstation. "You're absolutely right." I wiped off the board.

"What are you doing?" Loretta cried out. "I need your help. I might be a suspect."

"Fiddlesticks." I shook my head at Loretta then gave Aunt Maxi a subtle wink when she started to open her mouth. "I'm sure the inspector didn't check out those old ropes and Spencer is right. We are just being busybodies like we always are."

That seemed to settle Mark down a little. He put his bag on the stool seat and took out his notebook.

"I'm going to finish up my article for today, and I wanted to get a statement on what you saw today. That's why I'm here." Mark opened the notebook and clicked the top of his pen, ready for the statement.

"You can actually grab that from the police report." I smiled, grabbing the thawed maple glazed long johns. "I've got customers. I'm sure you understand."

I hurried out the kitchen door with the platter. While I was putting them into the display case, I was happy to see out of the corner of my eye that the three of them had filed out of the kitchen. I'd also gotten a text from Crissy.

According to the message, the bag had come down on her shin bone, bruising it badly but not breaking her leg. She said she'd be here this afternoon for the girls' meeting about Emily's see-you-later party and told us not to start without her. She texted that she had some really great ideas for the girls, and that made me a little nervous.

Crissy's great ideas were far from my great ideas. Maybe we could meet in the middle somewhere. I didn't have time to worry about that now that I knew she was okay, so I turned my attention back to the group standing in the middle of my kitchen.

Mark, of course, didn't think anything of my sudden change of heart. He had stopped when he saw Perry Zella and his mystery group at the middle table of the coffee shop.

"What was that about?" Aunt Maxi had dragged Loretta over to the counter. "You know as well as I do that Alan was murdered. It's just gonna take time for Spencer to figure it out. And we could be suspects." She gestured between her and Loretta.

"And so could he." I slid my gaze to Mark Redding. "Think about it. He and Alan had the most public fights, and it was no secret Alan despised him. Not to mention how each said to the other that they could end each other's career."

"Oh." Loretta's eyes grew as big and round as her lips. "You are so good."

"Top in my class for body language." It was true.

It was taught in law school how very important it was to be able to read body language, and I ended up being very talented in that department.

"Mark Redding's body language told me he knew more about what happened than he's letting on. Maybe he's not the killer, but he knows something." My brow rose, and I shut the display case.

The bell over the door dinged. A smile as big as the day was long grew across my face, and my heart went pitter-patter when I saw it was Patrick.

I watched him weave in and out of the tables, shaking the hands of the folks he knew before he made it to me.

"Can I talk to you? Privately?" he asked after he gave Aunt Maxi a hug and patted Loretta on the arm.

"Listen here." Loretta leaned into him. "If I'm a suspect, I expect your wife to help me."

"Suspect?" He laughed. "Suspect in what?"

"Gossip," Aunt Maxi said and jerked Loretta's sleeve. "Let's go grab a coffee."

Aunt Maxi knew Patrick so well that she knew if he even heard I was sticking my nose into another murder investigation, he just might lose it or I just might lose him.

"Listen, I've been thinking about the idea of the roastery, and I think we can do it. I called Tamara. She said that it just might work out, and I'm going to meet her this afternoon. I called Emily, and she can too." He stopped talking and gave me a shifty look. "What's wrong?"

It didn't take Patrick long to look around the coffee shop and then at Aunt Maxi before he knew something was up.

"There are a lot of people here that aren't normally here at this time." He pointed at Loretta and Aunt Maxi. "I thought they had rehearsal."

The door of the coffee shop swung open like the curtain was rising on opening night before Gretchen Cannon walked in, the fur coat draped over her forearm. She handed it off to Sydney.

"You simply have to get this cleaned." She stomped back with me in her sight and used a very loud outside voice, putting all eyes on her.

"Now that Sydney has looked at the script, she's going to. . ." Gretchen hesitated and made the sign of the cross, the first inclination the woman even believed in the big guy in the sky. She dabbed her eyes with the handkerchief and stumbled over her words. "I just can't. I can't. Simply can't." She motioned at Sydney.

"She simply can't believe Alan is gone." Sydney held the fur out over the counter for me to take.

"Gone? Y'all ran him off already?" Patrick laughed and looked around to see our reactions. "What? Y'all act like someone died."

"And I thought southern men were supposed to be gentleman," Gretchen scoffed and marched toward the door.

"Here." Sydney thrust the big fur coat at me and then took off after Gretchen.

"What was that?" Patrick stood there with a dumbfounded look on his face.

"Alan is dead," I whispered over the counter with the darn coat in one hand. I picked up one of the maple glazed long johns and practically stuffed the entire thing in my mouth.

"You literally ate that in one bite, which tells me you are stressed. Kitchen. Now." He pointed to the kitchen and took off in that direction.

"What am I going to do with this fur coat?" I asked Bunny.

"Perry Zella is right over there. Maybe his laundromat can clean it." She made a very good suggestion.

Perry and the mystery group were discussing Alan with Mark when I walked up.

"I'm sorry to interrupt, Perry, but do you think you could clean this fur for me? Coffee was spilled on it, and I believe they need it for the play." I tried to look around the darn thing for the coffee stain but couldn't find it.

"No problem. I can have it ready tomorrow afternoon."

"Great. That's great news." I pointed to the coat rack next to the front door. "I'll put it over there so you can grab it on your way out."

"Sounds good. I'll see you tomorrow afternoon," he told me and went back to his group while I headed back to the kitchen.

"Let me guess." Patrick didn't leave me any space to explain about Alan before he started in on me. He began the usual lecture I got when he didn't approve of me doing a little snooping around. "You think he was murdered. The whiteboard gave it away."

"In Roxy's defense…" Loretta Bebe had pushed her way into the kitchen and the conversation. "If Alan's death is ruled a homicide, I will be a suspect, Patrick. I don't do well in jail." She gnawed her lip. "Not that I've ever been in prison, but I don't do well under high stress. I start breaking out in hives." She started to scratch.

"Who does she think she's fooling?" Aunt Maxi had also joined us. "Unfortunately, there's no tanning bed in prison, so she's worried we'll all find out she's been lying all these years," Aunt Maxi said in a hushed tone while Loretta did her best to convince Patrick she needed my expertise in the law field.

"Thank you, ladies, but I think I'll talk to Patrick alone." I gestured for them to leave us alone and turned around to face him when they were safely out of earshot. "We aren't sure if he was murdered or not."

"How did he die?" Patrick asked.

While I told him the entire story, I grabbed some Kentucky burgoo from the freezer and part of today's lunch special since it was pretty near time for the lunch crowd.

"And you have already declared it a murder even though Spencer hasn't claimed it to be a murder?" Patrick shook his head.

"I'm claiming it now." Spencer walked into the kitchen. "Roxy, I'm going to need your full statement because after we inspected all the ropes and the rope in particular that snapped and gave Alan his fatal blow, it was cut, and the knife was found on the catwalk."

Spencer pulled out his phone and showed me a few photos.

"Geez." Patrick ran his hands through his hair. "You're not going to try to solve this. Tell her, Spencer. Tell her to stay out of this one."

"I'd like to do that, Patrick, but one problem." Spencer slid his gaze to me. "You're our only witness to someone being up there, and I'm afraid if they saw you looking up at them, you could be in danger."

That startled me into a wide-eyed expression.

CHAPTER TWELVE

$\mathcal{I}$'d like to say Patrick's attitude turned around after Spencer gave me a time to be at the department to give my statement, but it didn't. One, he was mad because it was the same time he wanted me to meet with Emily and Tamara. Two, he didn't want me to be the next victim. He remembered other circumstances when my big nose got me into a situation in which someone had literally set my cabin on fire to keep me from snooping.

Of course I'd spent twenty minutes trying to convince Patrick I was safe and it was all good. Then he got a text from Walker Peavler, Camey's husband. They wanted to know if we wanted to come to the Cocoon Hotel for dinner. A little couple's night.

It was a no-brainer for me that I wanted to go since I knew I wanted to get the scoop on what Alan and Gretchen had been arguing about so loudly, according to Mark.

Patrick was going to meet with Tamara without me and afterwards take Pepper home for me.

Still, I couldn't wait to get to the sheriff's department to talk to Gloria Dei, one of the employees of the department. She wasn't a deputy, just a secretary who knew it all.

Though it was Bunny's afternoon to stay before the afternoon gals relieved her, I told her to go on home because there was really no sense in me leaving. When the afternoon staff arrived, it would be time for me to head on over to the department, then come back to meet with the girls about Emily's see-you-later party.

The first building on Main Street was the Honey Springs Church. I couldn't stop the memories of when Patrick and I were teenagers. Both our families made us go to church, but little did they know that we'd slip out the back door before Sunday school started. We weren't doing anything bad, just acting like two teenagers who liked to spend time down on the shore of Lake Honey Springs. Aunt Maxi said that if I didn't watch it, I was going to lose my religion on that lake. I didn't know what she meant at the time.

Next to the church were the firehouse and the sheriff's department, where I needed to be. Across the street from that was the Moose Lodge. I pulled in the only free spot that looked to have been cleared from the snow and headed to the front door of the department, but not before grabbing the box of sweet treats and a thermos of coffee.

I rarely went anywhere without taking some coffee and sweet treats. Especially the department, where the treats not only helped me get information out of Gloria but also out of the deputies. Not like they'd come out and tell me something on purpose, but coffee and treats did make people chat and get them to say things they normally wouldn't just blurt out.

"Roxy!" Gloria rushed over to me when I walked in. "I was supposed to get off at three, but I saw on the ledger of the Bogart file you were coming in." Her eyes drew to my hands. "Are those...?"

"Treats." I smiled and handed them to her.

"Not that I was waiting around for those, but I will have one." She gestured by nodding for me to follow her over to the small table, where the coffee pot carafe was completely stained around the glass pot where the hours-old coffee had sat without being dumped. "The deputies are great at their jobs, not great at coffee."

"That's why you have me." I patted her on the back. "So you've seen the Alan Bogart file?"

"Mm-hmm." Gloria was busy looking into the bag of goodies I'd brought before deciding on one of the cranberry scones with the sparkling hard sugar crystals on top. "Let me tell you, no one was more surprised than Spencer when the forensic team came back with the rope in the evidence bag."

"I'd like to get a look at that rope." I wasn't so subtle.

"I knew you were going to say that, and I can't get over how you are the only witness." She took a bite and glanced around the department. "Spencer had to go back to the theater for a second because I'd heard there was another piece of evidence they wanted him to see on the catwalk, so I'm going to go tell the deputies there's a few goodies out here, which might take me a few minutes."

I followed her eyes as they shifted from me to the yellow file on her desk.

"Gotcha." I winked and smiled, since this was how she and I danced around her not showing me the file but telling me it was on the desk.

Granted, I could get a hard talking-to if I got caught looking through the file, but if I got caught taking photos of anything in there, then that'd be a whole other story.

Which I did. I had taken out my cell phone and took a photo of the file's photo of the severed rope. Even though it might have appeared to be just a cut rope, the way the fibers were cut would be able to tell a real forensic team exactly what type of tool was used to cut it. The murder weapon was definitely the sandbag, but the tool used to cut the cord would probably lead us to Alan's killer.

There wasn't a whole lot in there that blew my mind or that I didn't expect to see in an initial autopsy report Kevin had performed. Alan Bogart's death had been caused by a broken neck. Kevin had ruled it instantaneous, which gave me a little bit of relief since Alan didn't even see it coming. For that, I was grateful.

In the file there appeared to be next of kin, and it was marked that they'd been contacted. I couldn't get to the dictation of the conversation, since the sounds of chatter and feet were coming back down the hall.

"Roxy, glad to see you got here on time." Spencer was with the group. "I was a little surprised when Gloria told me you were here and alone with the file." He grabbed the file from Gloria's desk. "Not that I'm accusing you of looking at it, but I'm not putting it past you either."

"Spencer," I said with a gasp. "Me? Unethical? I'm just sitting here twiddling my thumbs."

"Roxanne Bloom, twiddling her thumbs when there's been a murder." He scoffed. "Y'all hear that?" His questions were met by a few nods along with some laughs from the deputies, who'd already started to munch on some goodies and make themselves a cup of coffee.

"Ha, ha." The sarcasm was in my tone.

"I actually asked you down here to talk about exactly that. Follow me." He waved the file at me to come with him.

There was a nice long silent pause between us. Another technique I learned in law school. So many times people talked through awkward silences or pauses, but if you could just beat the silence and not give in, the other person would start talking. I didn't want to add anything to my conversation with Spencer at all. He was the law, and anything I said could be held up in court. I was on an answer-only basis with him at this point in the investigation.

He took me into an interrogation room I'd been in before. I sat down in the chair before he even asked me to and watched him get all the equipment together.

"I'm glad Crissy is going to be okay." He set up the microphone and recorder before he planted himself in the chair.

"Me too," I said and watched him open the file, take out his little notebook, and click his pen.

"State your name, occupation, date of birth, and why you were at the theater." He knew he didn't need to tell me why we were here. It was the official statement he needed for the investigation now that Alan's death was ruled a homicide.

I told him the story of how someone's movement caught my eye when I was helping Aunt Maxi up to her feet where I'd knocked her out of the way, followed up by my noticing someone going through the door. Then Spencer turned off the tape recorder.

Interesting.

"You're our only witness." He said it again, but his tone was different from when he'd first mentioned this at the coffee shop. "I didn't want to talk about it in front of Patrick because I know how touchy he is when you get a little too involved. But it's been brought to my attention that none of these people get along."

He pulled a piece of paper out of the file I'd not been able to flip to.

"I also know they've all been to the coffee shop." He pointed at the photos of all the suspects I had in my mind. "I talked with Alan's production crew. All of them have worked with Alan for a long time, and they all know how he works. According to them, they know exactly how he likes everything set up, and when they were putting up the overhead lights for the production, there weren't any sandbags up on the catwalk or overhead. I've been trying to get in touch with Butch Turner to get a copy of the last inspection, since Loretta Bebe kept saying it had passed."

"You're beating around the bush." I could tell he was circling around to get to why I was really here. "Just cut to the chase."

"Fine." He sucked in a deep breath and looked cautiously at me, as if he were trying to assess whether to ask me something or tell me what he wanted to tell me. "I wanted to see if you could get any information out of these people at the coffee shop or just keep your ear to the ground. I was going to put someone on you since I'm worried that the killer saw you, but if we don't come out and publicly say we have a witness, then I think you'll be safe. Besides, I don't think you'd let me put someone on you, and I know if I told you Loretta Bebe was in fact a suspect, you'd end up helping her in some shape or form." His shoulders relaxed as he got the words out. "So I might's well use you to my advantage and get a report on what you hear so we can get this thing solved."

"Spencer Shepard." A big grin crossed my lips. "You do think I'm pretty good at solving crimes."

"Now, now. Don't be thinking you're getting a gun or badge," he joked. "Honestly, it's not looking great for Loretta. Especially since we have two witnesses who she told if she'd known he was going to change the script, she'd rather he'd crawled in a hole and died. They also mentioned some sort of verbal fight between the two." Spencer took out his phone and laid it on the table. "And without internet, we've got to go back to good ol' foot-and-mouth investigation."

"The internet is still out?" That was more shocking than Loretta being a suspect.

"Yep." He shook his head. "We rely on emails, cross-references, and even looking up phone numbers to call over agencies when we get a homicide. Those things are only found on the internet in this day and age. Really making it much harder and take longer to get to even the slightest bit of information needed for a murder investigation."

Spencer was right. We'd gotten so used to having technology at our fingertips and instant gratification that it took something like a big snowstorm that knocked out the internet to really get us back on our toes.

"Luckily for you"—I pointed at him—"I've never had the amazing technology you've had to figure out a couple of your investigations and had to rely on the sleuthing I know." I tapped my nose. "Being nosy, asking questions, and kinda doing things not on the up and up."

"Those are things I don't want to know, but I do want to know if you hear anything." He closed the file. "And are you sure you don't want someone in plain clothes to be hanging around in case the killer tries to come after you?"

I tilted my head to the side, with my jaw relaxed and an eyebrow tugged up.

"Just had to make sure." He and I both stood up at the same time. "Who do you think did it?"

This was such a turning point in our relationship, and I was very excited about it. Given that he knew I was a lawyer, he knew I would be smart.

"I'm a little on the cautious side with Mark Redding."

Spencer flipped the file back open.

"He's the reviewer with the *Times*."

"Yeah, yeah." Spencer nodded. "I've got a call into the *Times* so I can get information on him from his boss. I can't even get things like background checks with the internet down. Warrants. Nothing."

"He's a talker. He's really gotten invested in Perry Zella's mystery club. I'll see what I can get out of Perry when I drop by there tomorrow to get *Gretchen Cannon's fur coat*," I said in a fancy tone of voice. I ran my hand down my front like I had on a fur coat.

"Don't be getting yourself into any situation that can harm you," Spencer warned.

"Don't worry. I love my life and am not ready for it to end." I pulled my phone out of my pocket and waved it over my shoulder on my way back down the hall. "I'll call you."

CHAPTER THIRTEEN

*N*ow that I had clearance from Spencer to stick my nose in places where it didn't need to be stuck, I was actually excited about getting the meeting with the girls over with and going to the Cocoon Hotel, where I would meet up with Patrick, Camey, and Walker for supper.

All my suspects were staying at the Cocoon, and someone had to have overheard something. The only problem I was going to have was Patrick. I'd rather face any killer than face Patrick. He'd have a conniption for sure if he knew Spencer had even asked me to snoop.

I had to put all my sleuthing ideas and questions away when I got back to the Bean Hive and found all the girls who would be going to Emily's see-you-later party were already there and having coffee and a dessert.

Crissy Lane, Camey Montgomery, Fiona Rosone, Joanne Stone, Kayla Noro, and Leslie Roarke had pushed together some tables and were too busy chatting to even notice I'd come in.

"How's business been?" I asked the young girl who worked for me in the afternoon.

"No one has come in until your friends. Then Camey brought the morning coffee carafes, and I washed those." She shrugged and then pointed at a schoolbook on the counter. "I've been studying for a test I have tomorrow."

"No internet still?" I asked, hoping it'd been restored in the few minutes' drive it took me from downtown back to the boardwalk.

"Nope, and it's making me anxious," she said.

"Don't be anxious. If you can't get on your social media, then none of your other friends can." I could see the anxiety starting to rise. "You can pack up and go on home. I'm going to close early, since no one will be out in this weather."

"You know it's not that I want to see what they are doing, but this week is the week we are all supposed to hear what college we got accepted into, and we're all pretty much competing for spots that are hard to get." She flipped her book closed. "I'm dying to know if I get in. The schools send out emails now instead of big packets in the mail. It's killing me not to have access to email."

"I'm sure you're going to get into all the schools you've applied to." I tried to assure her and put her at ease.

Even though she smiled, I could tell her mind was jumbled with her thoughts.

"There you are!" Camey hollered across the coffee shop. "Come join us. I think we've already got it planned."

"That's good." I did a quick sweep of the coffee shop to see what I needed to do before the girls left and I had to close up. "Hey, Mocha." I reached up on the top of the cat tree and gave her a few chin rubs and pulled away before she'd had enough.

"We've decided to get the room at the Moose Lodge and get a little bluegrass band." Crissy was no worse for the wear. She looked as good as ever. "I'm not going to be able to do much line dancing since I've got this nasty bruise."

"Yes." Fiona's eyes grew big. "I can't believe you were at this murder too."

Fiona had been a great witness for me in the last case I'd stuck my nose in, which just so happened to be a murder. One I'd like to forget about.

"I was telling Fiona that you needed to not think about a roastery and open up a private investigation office." Leslie Roarke caught me off guard.

"Who said anything about a roastery?" I questioned.

"Emily. When I asked her if anyone was interested in the space, she mentioned it." Leslie pulled a book out of her purse. "I brought this book from the bookstore about different roasteries in Kentucky."

"And I had a few reference books I'd pulled from the library but forgot them." Joanne Stone, the librarian, frowned as she twirled the braid she'd styled her long red hair into.

"Thank you," I told them both. "It's super-early stages of talking. It wouldn't make any sense if the roastery was a few doors down."

They all agreed but thought it was a great idea.

"What is this about the Moose?" I asked.

"We figured you could provide coffee. Fiona is going to see if the Watershed would give us a great deal on some simple finger foods. Camey said she and Walker could decorate and use some of the stuff they have in storage for the Cocoon Hotel." Crissy got confirmation from each of them. "We will all pitch in to pay and make sure we clean the Moose up afterwards."

"I'm going to get the band the Bee Farm uses during the summer tours." Kaya Noro was the owner of the Bee Farm, which was located on the island across from the boardwalk across Lake Honey Springs.

She had to use a boat to get across the lake to the mainland when she needed to come over.

"And we have internet." She was smiling so big. "I have no idea how we have it, but we do, and I'm dying to catch up on my Instagram, so I've got to get going."

"You are a very bad friend," I told her and held up a finger for her to wait before she left. "Camey, can you help me box up a few things for the girls to take home?"

"Sure." She readily agreed and got up to meet me behind the counter.

"Listen." I grabbed her arm. "I need to get some information about some of your guests, mainly Gretchen Cannon, Alan Bogart, Mark Redding." I snapped a finger. "And Sydney O'Neil."

"Are they suspects?" Her eyes glowed with excitement.

"To me they are. Spencer has pegged poor Loretta, who'll just die if she hears." I left out that Loretta had already mentioned to me she was worried they might make her a suspect.

"She'd just lie down and die herself rather than go to jail." Camey shook her head slowly and took the to-go box I'd given her.

"I'd heard there was some arguing going on this morning." I wanted to give her a little intro to what I wanted her to expand on.

"Some?" She drew back and sighed loudly. "I've not been the hostess I like to be as the hotel owner. I've traded my sweet and southern hospitality for a referee shirt." She scanned the display case and picked out a few more treats for each one of our friends to take home. "They are all at each other's throats, and I can't make heads or tails of it."

"The main body of one of the tails is dead." I filled another box and started to pick out more of the treats for another box. "Be sure to get some of the quiche in them too. I can't reheat those tomorrow, and these have been thawed from frozen."

Usually before Bunny left her shift, she was good at picking out the items that might go stale and taking them down to the church for the few homeless folks we did have in Honey Springs. Today she was just happy to get out, and I loved giving my treats to my friends when I could.

"I heard Gretchen was giving someone a fit." I didn't tell her how Mark had mentioned it, and she didn't ask.

"That woman treats everyone badly, and I don't see how they stand it. Coffee?" She pointed.

"Yeah. You can put as much of it in the to-go boxes as you'd like." I loved the boxes, which had nozzles and were big enough to serve eight people. "The afternoon girls are so good about making coffee for the after-supper coffee drinkers, but I don't think anyone is coming out tonight."

"You mentioned Gretchen. She had an argument with Alan, Sydney, and Mark this morning. If I was that assistant of hers, I'd quit."

"Sydney has a degree in film or something like that." I remembered hearing something about it in passing. "Gretchen even mentioned Sydney taking over production."

"What would be Gretchen's motive to have killed Alan?" Camey asked, just in earshot of Crissy.

"Oh! Are we trying to find Alan's killer?" Crissy bounced on her toes. "I loved when we did all that sleuthing last time."

We laughed at the memory of the three of us cramming into Crissy's VW Beetle. The laughter and merriment spread to the rest of the group, ending my conversation with Camey.

They were all happy to get the treats and take the coffee home. Camey said she'd see me in a couple of hours for our couples dinner date, which would give me time to get the coffee shop ready for tomorrow morning, but instead I had a different idea.

"Kayla…" I stopped Kayla on her way out. "Do you mind if I hitch a ride over the lake and use your internet?"

"You're sleuthing again, aren't you?" Her brows arched.

"You know it." I laughed, remembering how I did help her and Andrew out once when they were in a bit of a pickle. "I just can't let Spencer think Loretta killed that producer. Who knew the internet could really hinder a case?"

"You know I don't mind. In fact, it's exciting, and I'm so happy to help. I can even say I had a small part in your becoming a famous detective," she joked. "You ready?"

"Absolutely." I hurried over to Mocha and made sure she was okay. I also wanted to make sure she had plenty of food and water. "I will check the heat because we want her to be toasty."

"You don't have someone to adopt her yet? She's a doll." Kayla walked over to Mocha, and Mocha let Kayla pick her up.

Mocha batted at Kayla's shiny brown hair, which had Medusa-like waves. She had on her typical Bee Farm tee, tucked into her khaki pants, showing off exactly how tiny she was.

Mocha was becoming very comfortable with people touching her, and I loved it.

"She just got here, and then we had this crazy snowstorm, so not a lot of people have gotten to meet her." I turned up the heat a smidgen, checked the fireplace to make sure it had died down, turned on the radio for Mocha, and resigned myself to the fact that closing everything for the shop was going to have to wait until the morning.

It was my turn to open, and I wasn't sure where we stood on providing coffee and the pecan ring to Gretchen, so I made the administrative decision to simply shut the lights off, lock the door, and head on over to the Bee Farm island to use Kayla's internet.

Both of us bundled up. It was cold on the boardwalk, but when we got out on Lake Honey Springs, it was going to be downright frigid.

All the shops on the boardwalk looked as though they were closed. It was the off season, and it was normal for most of us to close early, but this early was rare.

"I can't wait for all this snow to melt." Kayla led the way down the boardwalk to the ramp of the boat dock.

"I love Honey Springs in all the seasons but not this cold." I shivered just watching the wind whip up on the lake. Parts of the lake were frozen on top, and some parts weren't. "You can get your boat through that?"

"Oh no. Big Bib is really helpful when the lake is like this." She opened the door to the marina's shop. Big Bib was in there watching television and eating some chips from a bag.

"Hey, Roxy." A smile crossed his lips, though you couldn't see it under that big thick beard of his. "What are you doing here?"

He got up and grabbed the soft flotation key ring with a small boat key on it. When he stood, it showed off just how big and burly he was, true to his name. Granted, his legal name was Big, but it was also Bib. Around here, it wasn't unusual to go by two names or even a nickname. Nickname in Big Bib's case.

"I'm going to head over to Kayla's for about an hour and a half." I pointed at Kayla's box. "I've got some goodies for you if you'd come back and get me then."

"You are awful." Kayla simply laughed and opened the box. "But I understand these tasty treats can persuade anyone to do anything. That's Roxy's secret weapon."

"And a mighty good one too." He looked in the box, rubbed his hands together, and reached in for a maple glazed long john.

"Here." Kayla put the box of long johns and the box of coffee on the counter. "I don't need all those calories. You can have the whole box."

"What about Andrew? He might want some." Big Bib was trying to be nice, but it was written all over his face how much he wanted all the goodies.

"No way. He needs to watch his sugar intake." Kayla shook her head. "He's already eating too much honey."

"We better get going." Big Bib grabbed a handful of pecan balls and then gestured for us to follow him to the boat ramp, where one of his boats was tied up snug to the dock. "Be sure to grab a life jacket." He popped a couple of the balls in his mouth.

Kayla and I helped each other adjust the straps, tugged the life vests over our coats, and snapped them into place. Meanwhile, Big Bib revved up the engine and untied us from the slip.

The lake was a little rocky and choppy. I held on tight as he maneuvered the boat around some of the ice patches, and I kept my head down so I'd not get the brutal part of the wind in my face.

The engine slowed after ten minutes. I looked up, and Bib was steering us right on into Kayla's dock at a perfect angle. He was so good at getting the boats in slips the first time. It would take me several attempts of backing up and pulling forward before I'd ever get it just right. Not Big Bib. He was perfect each time.

During the summer months when the Bee Farm was open for tours and tasting, Big Bib made great money as the only type of transportation for tourists who didn't have a boat docked at his marina.

Even in the dead of winter, visiting the Bee Farm was amazing. It took up the entire island. There were many trails and different stops along the way, and Andrew had posted signs there about which bees lived where. They had devoted the entire island to the species and taking care of the ever-dying bee population.

During the warmer months, Andrew and Kayla had a nice building on the island with a unique roof shaped like a honeycomb, which was a perfect place for tourists to take selfies. On most summer nights they had a live band playing while the tourists enjoyed the various honey-tasting stations. There was a small store where Kayla and Andrew sold fresh honey.

It was the only honey I used for the Bean Hive. I was happy to promote other local businesses.

"Thanks." Kayla handed Big Bib some money. "Don't forget tomorrow."

"I won't." He stuck the money in the pocket of his heavy Carhartt jacket. "I'll be back to get you in about an hour and a half."

"Sounds good." I took his hand and let him help me off the boat while Kayla grasped the edge of the boat, keeping us butted up to the dock.

She and I waved goodbye to him while he pushed the boat's gear into reverse and manipulated it around some more ice.

"He's so good at that." I couldn't help but bring it to her attention. "Just like we are all good at our jobs. This entire island is amazing. Even in the snow."

"Andrew does most of it by himself. Crazy." Kayla headed off down one of the many trails the island had and that they'd made as part of the tourists' tours. "Our house is this way."

The trail was amazing. It wasn't one I'd ventured down before, since it truly wasn't marked as one for tourists because it led up to their private property. The snow along the trail must have been patted down with some sort of machine—I noticed there were tracks. It was too cold to ask or talk, so I observed as we walked along.

Tall evergreen trees lined each side of the path, and before too long, we came to a bridge that crossed over a small creek.

"This is my favorite spot." Kayla had stopped midway across the bridge. "Andrew built this bridge all by hand. He used dead trees and salvaged what pieces of wood he could. He made all these boards and crafted it." A big smile curled up on her face. "It's where he proposed."

"I love it. So romantic," I said with a sigh and took in a nice deep breath of the chilly air. "How did you get the island?"

"Andrew and I grew up here. He inherited it from his grandfather because his parents live really close to your Aunt Maxine, but they didn't want to live on the island." She started to walk again. "Sometimes during these months, we can't get off the island, and we still have to tend to the bees. Andrew was the only one who truly cared so much about them that he went into the family business, and all his family is thrilled."

"You? You don't mind being alone all out here when you know you can't get across the lake?" I asked because I knew it would drive me crazy.

Even if I didn't really need to leave the house, knowing I couldn't would make me want to.

"We have so much to do around here I don't even notice. And we have plenty to keep us occupied." She winked, given the romantic scene.

"Yeah. Still..." I hesitated. "I'd go nuts."

"Nah. You'd just make more coffee."

The trail opened into about an acre of flat land. Their cottage house was located in the middle.

"Isn't that amazing?"

"Wow," I literally gasped at the picturesque sight of their little yellow cottage house with its sloping snow-covered roof and the woods surrounding their property. All the trees had a nice layer of snow on the branches.

"See, I don't mind being iced in." She gestured for me to follow her. "Let's go inside and get some coffee and on the computer."

The inside of the cottage was much larger than it appeared from the outside.

"The cottage was Andrew's grandparents'." Kayla and I sat down on the small bench just inside of what was pretty much a log cabin. "They wanted the look of a cottage on the outside but used much of the wood and resources from the woods on the inside."

Kayla took off her shoes and walked over to the kitchen. I took off my shoes and let her make the coffee while I toured around the open space.

"Crazy how I have never been back here." I looked out the back window and noticed another small house that was in the woods. The insides glowed a warm yellow from the lights. "What's back there?"

"That's another house we have for the bees." Kayla made all sorts of noise in the kitchen, but I was too busy looking out at the landscape and watching for Andrew's shadow to pass across the window of the other little cottage to pay her any attention. "Instead of furniture, it's all the bee houses."

"It's amazing out here." I turned around when I heard her walking towards me. "I could probably be okay out here in an ice- and snow-storm now that I've seen it."

"Too bad you gave away our sweet treats or we could have had one with the coffee." She handed me the laptop from her hands. "I'm joking."

"I know you are. But when he brings you back tomorrow, you stop in the coffee shop, and I'll have a new box ready for you to bring home."

"You can just open it up. We don't have the internet password protected because no one is out here to worry about."

I took the laptop over to the couch, opened the computer like she said, and clicked on the browser icon.

"I just can't get over you having the internet." I was tempted to check my email and a couple of my social media accounts but held off because I only had a limited time until I had to catch my ride back across the lake.

"It's crazy how well Andrew's grandfather could see far into the future and the property, how he really did build an amazing electric and data system. So we've never had an issue." She worked around the room while I started to type, starting my investigation of who the killer could possibly be.

"Gretchen Cannon." I typed her name, and the search engine brought up her IMB account with all her details and biography on it.

Nothing in there made me pause, so I hit the back arrow to scan down the results from the search.

My eyes scanned down the page. There weren't any glaring words that stood out until… I arrowed over to the next Google search page and saw Alan Bogart's name in the text. I clicked on the highlighted link.

There were several articles about a romance between Alan and Gretchen along with some paparazzi photos.

"Oh my," I said with a gasp.

"Find something?" Kayla hurried over to the couch with two cups of coffee in her hands. She set them down on coasters and sat next to me. Then she looked at the screen where I had pointed out the article.

"Gretchen Cannon and Alan Bogart had a romance." My jaw dropped. I looked at Kayla with wide eyes.

"Scorned love is a great motive for a murder," she said in a singsong voice. "Click on the images."

When I did that, all sorts of photos popped up, citing various articles.

"I was thinking the same thing about scorned love. Let me see what it says about the breakup." I Googled their names and added "breakup" to the search.

"There's one." Kayla was so excited. "Click it." She picked up a coffee and handed it to me while we both sipped on them and read the article.

"According to this, they had a public fight and broke up. It doesn't say who did the breaking up, but it definitely is weird they'd be doing a play together here." I took another drink. "In fact, she owed him a favor. Trust me, if I was in an argument with someone as public as this… I don't think I'd be fulfilling any sort of favor."

"Is there any article saying they made up—or any articles about them since this one was published because this was five years ago?" Kayla had a good point. "A lot can happen in five years."

"I'll switch the filter on the search engine to the newest information." I changed the filter and hit Enter, but nothing came up as current or even from the last three years. "This was three years ago at some award ceremony."

We sat next to each other on her couch with our coffee mugs in our hands, reading the article.

"It says they went to great lengths to ignore each other," Kayla pointed out in the article. "What was the favor?"

"I don't know, but I'm going to try to find out." I exhaled a deep breath. "What about Mark Redding?"

"The paper guy?" Kayla asked.

"Yes. Alan despised him. They had a few public fights here and there." The one in the coffee shop as well as the one in the theater right before Alan was murdered stood out. "I'm going to see if there's anything on these two."

I set the mug back down on the coaster and typed in both of their names. Instantly, a legal document I was very familiar with popped up as the first thing, which told me it was the most searched document pertaining to the two.

"What is that?" Kayla pushed back her long hair over her shoulder as she leaned into the screen.

"It's a restraining order." I knew the form pretty well from when I was a lawyer on divorce cases. My client was either serving one or being served. "Good grief." I shook my head as I read through it. "Alan had a restraining order against Mark."

I scrolled down to check out the details of the length and the terms.

"The end date was a year ago, and it looks like Alan didn't go back in time to renew it." Most restraining orders contained a grace period of time in which they could go back to court and get the documentation and reason for the restraint without going through the whole ordeal. The judge would either grant the extension of the order or void the order altogether.

When I typed in more necessary information in the search engine, it appeared the order had run out and Alan was no longer restricted to the terms.

"Does it say why Alan had one on Mark?" Kayla asked.

"Let me see." I toggled back to the restraining order and scrolled down. "As if it couldn't get worse." I shook my head and read. "Apparently they were at one of Alan's rehearsals, and it was a medieval play."

I read ahead so I could summarize what I was reading to her.

"They had a fight, and Mark picked up one of the axes and swung it at Alan. Alan was in fear of his life and didn't want Mark anywhere near his productions." I blinked a few times and reread the conditions of the restraining order.

Quickly I typed in their names with keywords such as "feud," "reporter," and "legal documents."

"Look here." I used the cursor to point to the one article that said Mark was let go from his job as theatrical reviewer because of producer Alan Bogart's restraining order held against him. "And that is a motive."

"You think?" Kayla asked in a sarcastic tone. "I think I'll just stay on my own little island with Andrew and the bees. I'm happiest here."

"Do you have any vacancies?" I joked. "All kidding aside, I wonder why Alan didn't petition to extend the order. If someone came at me with an axe, I sure would make sure they didn't come near me again for the rest of my life."

"You've talked to Mark, right?" Kayla asked.

"I've talked to him here and there. A few conversations, but he made it seem like he was the victim of Alan's rants and that it was really Gretchen and Alan who had the biggest beef." I snapped my fingers when I remembered him coming to the coffee shop today. "He came in the Bean Hive, and I started to make a suspect list. He was very interested. Then I pretended to get busy so I could have him leave." I shook my finger in the air. "I had a feeling he didn't need to be there, but I'm still not sure I get 'killer' from him. Gretchen, she's a whole other story. Evil seeps out of her."

"How so?" Kayla asked and leaned back into the couch.

I set the computer on the coffee table and joined her with my coffee in hand.

"She has no regard for others' feelings. She's not nice to her assistant. She is demanding, and if she doesn't get her way, she lets you know it. And she stormed in here like this was her production and a play written just for her."

All the not-so-pretty sides of Gretchen twirled around in my head, making me wonder if she was the one who killed Alan.

"Think about it." My eyes slid over the rim of my mug as I took another drink. "She and Alan had a very public breakup. They were seen at an event three years ago where their people had made special arrangements for them not to interact, and then she shows up here because she's cashing in a favor?"

"Or was it her opportunity to murder him in this small-town play?" Kayla's eyes narrowed. "It's almost time for Big Bib to get you."

"Do you have a printer?" I asked.

"Shoot. That's the one thing I was going to pick up. Printer paper. We are out, but I'll get some tomorrow." She and I stood up. "What do you need?"

"I wanted to print off a few of these articles to give to Spencer. It can wait. Maybe the internet will be up tomorrow." I crossed my fingers in the air and got my coat and boots back on before I backtracked to the boat dock, where Big Bib was already waiting for me.

CHAPTER FOURTEEN

*T*here wasn't much chitchat between Big Bib and me because it was too dang cold and my breath would've frozen in mid-air.

Cocoon Hotel was a sight to behold from the water.

The historic white mansion that was built in 1841 had been in Camey's family for years. Camey had hired Cane Construction to help rebuild the old structure into an amazing hotel that was situated right on Lake Honey Springs and was able to keep the cozy character. The two-story white brick with the double porches across both stories was something to behold. It was difficult not to gasp out loud when it came into view. It was that spectacular.

It would be a perfect cover for any issue of one of those southern magazines you'd see while standing in the checkout line at the local grocery store.

"Here's your stop," Big Bib joked after he'd safely pulled into a slip, tied off, and shut down the engine.

"Thank you, sir." I couldn't help but smile at him. He looked so scary under his big burly size and that beard of his, but he was a teddy bear underneath. And someone who'd do anything for you. "Do you have a time you're going to get Kayla tomorrow?"

"Nah. She usually texts me." He put his hand out for me to take as he helped me off the boat. "You need something?"

"I might have to go back over and didn't want to create too much of a fuss." I walked alongside of him on the wooden dock towards the front of the marina. "I'll ask her in the morning."

"Where you off to?" Big Bib asked when I took a left to take the path to Cocoon.

"I'm going to have supper with Camey and Walker. Enjoy your treats." I snuggled my hands in the pockets of my jacket and hurried down the path toward the hotel.

It would be nice to have dinner with friends. Patrick and I rarely did it, since he was busy running Cane Construction and I was busy at the Bean Hive. Tonight was going to be nice—getting out of the rut of going back to the cabin and trying to figure out what was for dinner, since I cooked and baked and served coffee all day. Though I loved doing all those things for Patrick, sometimes it was just something I didn't want to do at night.

I'd hit the jackpot with Patrick. He could always tell when I was exhausted, and he'd come up with some sort of alternative. Like tonight.

Camey had also hit the jackpot with Walker. He'd come to town on business, and when he and Camey locked eyes... it was all she wrote. They were smitten with each other. She had bent over backwards to make his stay at the Cocoon Hotel a very nice and memorable one. So much so that he upped and moved to Honey Springs and brought Amelia, his granddaughter, who he had custody of, with him.

All in one big swoop, Camey had the instant family she'd always wanted.

It truly was a perfect union. He and Camey were both in their fifties, and Honey Springs was a fantastic place to raise a child. Camey, Walker and Amelia were one big happy family. Tourists always referred to Camey and Walker as Amelia's parents.

Amelia would smile and not dare correct them. She treated Camey and Walker as if they were her biological parents. And Camey treated the little girl as if Camey were Amelia's mom and loved her as such.

Camey had decided to keep her last name when they got married because of her business but recently had said how much easier it would be for Amelia and school documentation if they all did have the same last name. She'd never mentioned what solution they'd come to, so I should probably ask and check on my friend.

"My goodness," I blurted out when I saw Newton Oakley out with a dry paintbrush, brushing the snow off some purple type of plant. "What on earth grows in this type of weather?"

The wheelbarrow was full of shovels, spades, and all sorts of gardening tools I didn't even know the name for but recognized. Gardening was not my thing. My thumb was not green, nor did I have the desire to make it such.

"Cold-hardy camellias." He had pride written all over his face. "Maybe not the ice but in snow. I make sure I come out here every day during the snow and uncover them to make sure the investment Camey put into them is a good investment."

"You have so much joy in your work, Newton. I need to remember that when I make terrible coffee." I jogged up the steps with the warmth of the inside in my head.

"Now, now, Roxy. Your job brings a lot of joy to people around here —and warmth. Literally." He laughed and went back to using the dry paintbrush to carefully sweep the snow off.

The inside of the Cocoon was just as gorgeous as the outside. To the left of the big entry was the guest counter for check-ins and anything else guests needed. To the right was a huge room that Camey had turned into the hospitality lounge. It was also where I supplied her daily complimentary coffee and a few sweet treats for her guests.

The crackling fire could be heard over some laughter. When I peeked my head inside the room, I was pleasantly happy to see the laughing was coming from my group.

"Roxy!" Patrick smiled and put his cocktail glass on the table. He hurried over to kiss me and help me out of my coat. "Get over there in front of the fire to warm up. You look like you're freezing."

"I am." I took Patrick's advice. I hugged Camey and Walker when I passed them on the way to warm my hands in front of the fireplace. "I'm so glad we could do this."

"We are too." Walker reached over and rubbed Camey's back. "Amelia had dance lessons, and it's not our night to carpool, so we thought we could get in some good dinner."

"Speaking of all that, we better get to the restaurant." Camey gestured for the men to lead, but she wasn't kidding me none. She wanted to scoop on what I found out.

"You won't believe it." I used my hand to cover a little of my mouth so Patrick couldn't hear because if he did, it'd ruin supper.

"Restraining order?" Camey gasped. "And they were both staying here." She did a quick jerk of the neck when we walked past the stairs that led up to the guest suites. "Spencer is up there now going through Alan's room. He even has a warrant to go through Gretchen's and Sydney's rooms."

"Really?" I was happy to hear Spencer was looking into other people besides poor Loretta. "I wish I could go tell him what I found on the internet, but it wouldn't go well with dinner."

"Internet? What did you find on the internet?" Walker asked. "You know you can't believe everything you read on the internet."

"But if it's on the internet, it has to be true." Patrick made Walker laugh with his comment.

"You two think you're so funny." Camey shrugged and led us through the restaurant bar to get us to her special table in a secluded room.

"If you'll excuse me for a second, I need to go to the bathroom." I smiled and tried not to look Patrick in the eyes because he'd know right away I was not telling the full truth, but I wasn't lying either.

I did have to go to the bathroom right after I talked to Sydney, who I just so happened to see sitting at the bar when we walked past her.

"What do you want?" Sydney's usual happy-go-lucky demeanor was a bit on the sour side. She picked up the glass and swigged down whatever was in it, and then she picked up her phone and tapped it a few times before she angrily smacked it on the bar top.

"The internet isn't working. Snowstorm." I shrugged and tried to break the ice between us.

"Of course. That's what we get when we come to these small towns." She rolled her eyes in disgust.

"Are you okay?" I asked and noticed the empty stool next to her.

"I'm fine. It's a Coke." She shook her head. "I don't drink. And if I did, I couldn't because you never know when Gretchen is going to need me."

"You must have a hard job." I sat down next to her and ordered a water when the bartender pointed at me. "I couldn't imagine the schedule you keep."

"She is demanding, but she's a great boss. I'm just tired of all the cops and people asking if she killed Alan. No way." Sydney was sure of it. "Alan and Gretchen had a long-running relationship."

"Yeah. I read somewhere they'd been romantically involved." I casually mentioned it, making Sydney laugh so hard she held on to the bar as if she were going to fall off the stool.

"That was a marketing ploy." Sydney smiled. "And you fell for it. See, it all works."

"Marketing ploy? You mean they did it for publicity?" I asked.

"Yeah. Alan's career was tanking, and Gretchen had just gotten that Tony Award. His people called her people. They all got together. Next thing I knew Gretchen's calendar was filled with dinner dates, a yacht date, and an airplane trip to nowhere just so the media would take photos of them to help jumpstart Alan's career."

"So that's the favor he owed her." I ran my finger along the rim of the glass of water and pondered what Sydney had said.

"Don't you dare tell her I told you. I just feel like I need someone to talk to now that we are going to stay here. If we wanted to leave, that cop guy said we can't." Her shoulders slumped. "I'm afraid they are going to arrest Gretchen because she honestly doesn't know how to stop arguing with people."

"You seemed to have mastered it." I wanted to give her some confidence. She looked defeated. "Not only do you cater to her, but now you're going to be doing the producing."

"As much of it as she'll let me. She's been rewriting the manuscript Alan had changed all day long. Of course making her part bigger, which she should. I'm not saying she shouldn't. She is the star, after all." Sydney thanked the bartender when the bartender slid a fresh Coke in front of her.

"What exactly was the favor Gretchen called in from Alan?" I decided to just go for it. I couldn't pretend I was in the bathroom all this time. I had to hurry and get to the point.

"Do you even know Gretchen's career?" Sydney asked.

"Honestly, I do not." I felt bad, but watching plays or even movies had never been my thing. "I was a lawyer, so my nose was always in a book."

"Wow." She jerked back. "That's cool. How did you go from that to making coffee?"

"See. Right there is why I need to open my roastery." I knew she didn't know what I was talking about. "I don't just make coffee. I actually roast it from the raw bean. It's an art. Like the theater."

"That's amazing. Can I stop by, since I'm stuck here, and see you do it?" She was all sorts of impressed, making me think the roastery was a great idea.

"I'd love for you to." I was always happy to talk about coffee. "So what were you saying about Gretchen's career?"

"She's always been the second leading lady. She's never gotten the big roles. She's good enough, but there's a chain of command, and she's not kissing no one's you-know-what to get her to the top." Sydney was alluding to all those rumors about directors and producers I'd recently seen on the news. "She'd rather get there by clawing her way to the top, so when she stopped getting a lot of calls for even the secondary roles, she knew it was time to cash in on the favor Alan owed her where she helped get his career back on track."

"I thought they hated each other." None of what Sydney was saying made sense. "They were always at each other's throats."

"In public, but are you kidding me? Just last night we were all in Gretchen's suite, watching a movie and eating popcorn. It was all an act, so Gretchen is upset about his death. That's why she'd vowed to make this the best play ever. She also made a deal with Mark to get it in all the papers for big reviews," Sydney muttered under her breath. "It's him that I'd be looking at if I were the cops."

"Sheriff." I finally corrected her.

"Huh?" she asked with a confused look.

"We don't have cops in Honey Springs. We have a sheriff's department." I waved my hand in the air to wave off her trying to understand it. "It's a county, city Kentucky thing."

"Oh." She looked off into the distance like she was trying to process my words.

"There you are." I felt someone's hand on my shoulder. "It's time to order."

"Oh, Patrick." Inwardly I cringed that I'd been there so long that he had to come looking for me. "This is Sydney O'Neal, Gretchen Cannon's assistant."

The two of them exchanged pleasantries.

"Are you coming?" he asked with a not-so-pleasant tone.

"Yeah." I slid off the stool. "Sydney, stop by the coffee shop anytime, and I'll roast some special beans just for us to enjoy."

"I'll do that." Sydney waved goodbye.

Patrick put his hand on the back of my arm.

"Where are your manners?" he scolded me like I was a child. "Our friends are hosting us for supper, and I'd like to think you were just exchanging hellos with that woman, but I know you all too well."

"Patrick, she's a guest of Camey's hotel and a customer of the Bean Hive. I wasn't going to be rude." I tried to answer as any good southern woman would. Turn the attention at hand to a mannered thing, and then any sort of underhanded reason I'd be talking with her would be forgotten, since it appeared as though I were being a good southern host.

"Roxanne Bloom Cane. I know you better than that, and I know for a fact you just can't stop sniffing around when there's a fresh murder down at Kevin's morgue."

"Keep your voice down." I shushed him, which he didn't like once we got to the table. "We will talk about this later."

"Talk about what later?" Camey asked and handed me the menu. "Try the glazed salmon. Tonight's special."

"I'll have that," I told the waitress, who was apparently waiting for me to return to the table to get our order. "We were discussing the murder of the producer because on my way to the bathroom, I noticed Sydney, Gretchen Cannon's assistant, sitting at the bar. I was simply checking in on her."

"Can you believe he was murdered?" Walker asked.

Poor, poor Walker. He had no idea what he'd just stepped into. Camey and Patrick both eased back in their chairs—Camey for reasons much different than Patrick. She knew he didn't want to discuss it, and he didn't want to discuss it.

"That reporter told me all about the restraining order that guy had against him." Walker started to tell the story of how he and Mark were having early-morning coffee when Mark just told him all about the fight they'd had.

Only Mark turned it around and made himself the victim, not Alan.

"How is Amelia doing in school?" Patrick abruptly changed the subject in a very nonchalant I-do-not-want-to-talk-about-the-murder way.

Camey kicked my shin under the table. I bit my lip not to cry out. It was her way of trying to be secretive about Patrick's behavior.

"She's doing..." Walker was a little apprehensive, as though he were trying to figure out Patrick's sudden attitude change.

"Great!" Camey's voice rose an octave. "She's gotten so involved with everything and keeping us busy."

"I can't thank Camey enough for taking such good care of her." Walker reached over and put his hand on top of Camey's. He looked at her with the most loving eyes. "I go out of town for work, and I am so thankful for her. I'm able to go on my trips knowing that Amelia is safe and happy, all because of this woman."

Patrick and I glanced at each other when Walker awkwardly leaned over and kissed Camey.

"Here we are." The waitress had brought the big tray of food out.

Each one of us pushed back from the table so she could put our plates in front of us. Most of the dinner was just chitchat about town but no mention of the murder or play. I knew if Camey had hit me under the table, she was probably doing the same thing to Walker.

It wasn't until Walker invited Patrick to look at the HVAC that Camey finally mentioned his odd behavior.

"And what was all that about?" She rubbed her cloth napkin over her mouth and laid it on top of her plate along with her knife and fork.

"When he came looking for me, I was sitting at the bar, talking to Sydney. He knows how interested I am in figuring out who killed Alan, but he's taken the stance that he doesn't want to know anything about it." I took a drink of the water and flipped the coffee cup over on the saucer for the waitress to give me a shot.

"He told you he didn't want to know?" Camey asked and flipped her cup over too.

"No. His actions told me. I mean, look at how he rudely didn't want to talk about it when Walker brought it up tonight." I gave a slight shake of my head when I saw the men coming back into the room with Amelia.

"Are you ready?" Patrick asked.

Amelia climbed up in Camey's lap. The love among the three of them warmed my heart so much. I was so happy to see that they'd come together.

"Camey." Newton walked in with a concerned look on his face. "I'm sorry to interrupt, but I was cleaning up to go home, and I noticed the ax is missing from my wheelbarrow. Did you borrow it?"

"No." Camey looked at Walker.

"I didn't take it." Walker looked back at Newton.

"I can't find it anywhere." Newton scratched his head. "The last time I used it was yesterday, when I cut down a few of the dead roots of a couple of bushes because they were too thick to use shears."

"Don't worry about it." Camey was so good at not stressing about too many things, a trait I wished I had. "I'm sure it'll turn up."

"If not, we can get a new one. Probably about time we replace a lot of your tools anyways." Walker brushed off the missing tool.

We all said our goodbyes.

"Do you want to ride with me and I can just bring you back in the morning?" Patrick asked.

"I'm going to open, since it's still so cold out." I forgot to text Bunny that I'd just open again. "I need to tell Bunny."

While Patrick and I walked in the cold to our cars, there was a frigid air between us, and I wasn't talking about the outside temperature.

To avoid it, I sent a text message to Bunny. After I sent it, I checked to see if there was internet.

"Oh. I think we've got internet." I quickly typed in Gretchen and Alan's names in the search engine, but the wheel of death continued to spin, which told me we didn't have the internet.

"I'm sorry." Patrick put his arm around me on our way to the parking lot.

"It's okay. We rely too much on the internet anyways." I slipped the phone back into my jacket pocket.

"No. I mean I'm sorry how I acted tonight." Patrick stopped in front of my car. "I know we can talk about this at home, but I worry about you. I know you're a lawyer. I know you have formulated all sorts of suspects in that little mind of yours. I love your mind. I love you, but it still doesn't keep you safe."

"I'm fine. You do worry too much." I wrapped my arms around him and looked up into his big brown eyes.

"Even Spencer said you were the only witness. That's what has been on my mind all day." He brought me closer to him and hugged me. "I don't know what I'd do if something happened to you."

"You don't need to worry about that. Let's get home and see the kids."

CHAPTER FIFTEEN

The wind whipped up during the night, waking me from a sound sleep. My mind started to wander, and Alan's murder played in my head, keeping me from falling asleep again. There was only another hour until my alarm went off, so I peeled back the covers and met Pepper in the family room.

He lifted his head from his dog bed in front of the fire, his ears bent back as if he were ready for me to say something to him.

"Hey, buddy." I squatted on the floor next to him and felt the warmth of the fire on my back.

It was a little too much excitement. He wanted more than a few rubs. He jumped into my lap with his front paws on my chest, doing his best to get in some good-morning kisses on my chin.

"You're such a good boy." My voice was a cross between a sigh and small giggle. "But it's time to get to work. I know it's early, but we have some sleuthing to do."

I would love to say he was eagerly excited about the sleuthing we were going to do by the way his tail was wagging, but he wasn't. He ran to his dog bowl and looked at it with the most pitiful eyes when he noticed there wasn't any kibble in it.

"Fine. I'll let you have some, and I'll make a coffee." I dumped enough kibble to hold him over until we got to the Bean Hive and brewed just enough coffee to hold me over until I got there.

In lickety-split time, I was showered and out the door before Patrick or Sassy even had time to roll over.

Pepper and I did our usual routine in opening the Bean Hive. Mocha had started to follow us around, which was a good sign she was getting comfortable. The knock at the door was a much-welcomed Emily Rich, who saw my light on early. She was going to the bakery to clean out the office.

"I heard the meeting went well between Patrick and Tamara." Emily reminded me that the meeting had totally slipped my mind.

"Oh brother. I was so wrapped up in Alan Bogart's murder investigation, I forgot to ask Patrick." A long sigh escaped me. "How could I be so selfish?"

"You? Selfish?" Emily shook her head and helped me get the coffee shop ready to open.

It was nice to have her there with me. She did work for me while she was in high school, so she could probably do it better than me.

"I don't know. You knew me as single Roxy. He's my husband, and I really should make it a point to ask him how his day is." I took out Mocha's food.

"Here. I'll feed her." Emily took the cat food and walked over to Mocha. Mocha meowed and rubbed up along Emily's leg.

"You know, she's putting her scent on you." I watched as Mocha continued to rub against Emily and dot her tail in the air, which was a sign of love. "She would make a great companion to someone who is moving to a new town."

"Oh no you don't." Emily wagged a finger at me. "I know what you're doing."

"I'm just making an observation. Trust me. I know." I reminded her that I was in her boat a few years ago, which was how Pepper came home with me.

"Let's talk about the murder. If Patrick won't listen, I sure will." Emily and I made our way back into the kitchen.

All the items were in the oven. The coffee was brewed, and soon it would be time to get the carafes ready for the Cocoon Hotel hospitality room.

"Well." I was all too happy to engage in what I'd discovered and eagerly grabbed the dry-erase board, propping it up on the prep table. "As I see it, we have three suspects. Only two, I think, had real motive."

I listed Loretta, Gretchen, and Mark.

"Loretta's only motive was that he changed the play on her. It did make her mad, and it bruised her ego a little, which made her talk bad about him, but you and I both know Loretta Bebe couldn't hurt a fly, much less a grown human man."

I moved on to Gretchen.

"Gretchen and Alan had pretended to be in a relationship when Alan's career was on the downward slide. They made sure they had public photos together and all sorts of appearances." I told her how Sydney had told me about it, and she'd know, since she'd been Gretchen's assistant. "She also told me how Gretchen agreed to it, and when she needed a favor, he'd have to give her one."

"I can see where this is going." Emily glanced over when my personal coffee pot beeped, having brewed a full pot. She walked over and made two cups of coffee while I continued the investigation into why I believed Gretchen could've been the killer.

"Gretchen's career is now on the way out. A has-been, like he said. So she called in her favor, which was..."

"To put her in the show." Emily finished my sentence with disbelief in her tone.

"When he changed the play, he also changed her role to a minor role as an old woman who gets killed." Emily and I both knew no woman liked to be called old. "Can you imagine what it's like to be an actress and have the industry not give you roles because they have dubbed you old?"

"Society already puts so many stipulations and opinions on us regular folk. I couldn't imagine if I were famous." Emily held the mug between her hands.

"Right? And Alan was public in calling Gretchen old." I didn't go into details or tell Emily the exact words, but she understood what I was saying. "Think about it. He moved her larger role to a smaller role, not only still keeping her career tanking but also hurting her overgrown ego."

Emily simply shook her head and drank her coffee while I wrote down all of Gretchen's motives underneath her name on the whiteboard.

"Then we have Mark Redding." I tapped his name with the marker tip. "Why? Why would a big-time reporter come here to our little town when there are so many big shows opening up on Broadway?"

"Umm… why?" Emily asked as though it were a trick question.

"Exactly." I smacked the counter. "Why? Well, he's getting back at Alan for putting the restraining order against him after Mark threw an ax…" My jaw dropped. "An ax. Oh no."

"What?" Emily watched me frantically feel around my body for my phone.

"Mark Redding is the killer," I called over my shoulder on my way out to the coat rack to get my phone out of the pocket of my coat. "Alan had a restraining order against Mark, but he let it go and didn't renew it. Mark had thrown an ax at Alan. Granted, it was a prop at a medieval play Alan was directing, but Mark did it."

I clicked on my photos and used my fingers to blow up the photo I'd taken of the evidence of the severed cord.

"Mark saw the ax in Newton's wheelbarrow, and he took it to the theater." I racked my brain while I paced back and forth in the kitchen. "Where was he when I went on stage right before Alan was killed? I don't recall seeing him, so he could've gone up on the catwalk with the ax, and that's when he cut the rope at just the right time—when Alan was standing under it."

"Ax? Newton's wheelbarrow?" Emily was so confused. "I have no idea what you are saying, but I'll take your word for it."

"Good. I've got to call Spencer." I took the casseroles out of the oven and replaced them with more goodies that just needed to be heated, then refreshed my coffee so I could sit down with my phone, call Spencer, and give him my full attention.

Emily got the carafe for the Cocoon Hotel together for me and decided she'd just go on and deliver it, telling me she'd talk to me later.

On the phone with Spencer, I went through the whole story from the internet search to the conversation I had with Sydney in the bar to the missing-ax story that ended my day of sleuthing. "I'm telling you, if you find the ax, you will find the fingerprints of Mark Redding," I told him.

"Kayla and Andrew have internet?" Spencer asked on the other end of the line.

"That's all you have to say after I just handed you the killer on a silver platter?" I asked.

"Thank you. I'll get it all checked out, but for now, I'm going to head over to the Bee Farm and get on their internet." Why didn't I think of that? "Keep your ears to the ground. Stay out of harm's way and let me know if you come up with anything else."

"Do you know when the internet is going to come back?" I figured he'd at least get some sort of sense.

"No. But I am planning on bringing this up at the next town council meeting. Honey Springs needs to invest in the fi-optics or some sort of internet that won't be taken out by a snowstorm. Ridiculous in this day and age." He seemed more upset about the internet than Alan's murder.

"Fine." I felt a little defeated. Spencer wasn't exactly as happy as I'd hoped he'd be, but maybe it was his way of trying to keep a level head.

Either way, I just knew Mark Redding had gotten his final revenge…and finished the job with a very fitting object… an ax.

CHAPTER SIXTEEN

"*A*n ax?" Aunt Maxi laughed from her dressing room when I told her about my theory. "Roxanne Bloom, you've lost your mind. The sandbag is what killed him."

"I know that, but someone had to have cut the cord." I showed her the photo on my phone.

I made sure I'd brought the coffee items and pecan roll over to the theater a little early so I could stop in and talk to Aunt Maxi. Bunny had gotten to work, and everything was done thanks to Emily, so it was easy leaving Bunny by herself for a little while.

"If what you said about Mark having a restraining order put on him by Alan because of an ax is true, I'd say you have something there." Loretta nodded.

"Did I hear someone say my name?" Mark Redding curled around the doorframe of the dressing room door. He had his big camera strapped around his neck.

"Where's the ax you cut the cord of the sandbag with?" Loretta was about as subtle as a screen door on a submarine.

"You think I killed Alan?" His brows furrowed. He looked up and down the hall before he stepped into the dressing room and shut the door behind him.

"What are you doin'?" Loretta took a couple of steps backwards. "You open up the door right this instant."

He lifted his finger to his mouth and said, "Shhhhhhh."

"I'm gonna scream," Loretta warned him. "You come a step closer."

"Seriously?" Mark didn't appear threatening, but I was cautious like Loretta.

"Why did you shut the door?" I asked.

"Because I don't want the real killer to hear us." He shrugged, putting his hands up.

"How do we know you're not the real killer?" Aunt Maxi asked. She'd picked up the pair of scissors in a stabbing hold, pointed it at Mark, and stepped in front of Loretta and me with her other arm out, motioning for us to get back.

"I told the *Times* people who are from here are crazy." He turned and put his hand on the doorknob like he was leaving.

"Crazy?" Oh… that set off Aunt Maxi, and that was a side you never wanted to be on. "Do you want me to show you crazy?"

"Listen." Mark jerked around. "Alan Bogart and I had our differences. We both love the theater and in the end knew that about each other. We still didn't like each other, but he knew I respected his work. That's why I'm here." He threw his hands in the air. "We had a fight. I threw a plastic ax at him. Plastic prop. The media made it out to be some sort of crazy moment, but it wasn't like that. Alan had to put a restraining order against me so he'd get good publicity. It's how it works when you're big time. Then I started to do reviews under a pen name, and it was all fine."

He pulled a card out from the camera case strapped on him and held it out.

"That's my pen name. Check it out." He laughed. "Not that I need to tell you three anything because the sheriff just left, and my alibi checks out. It must've been one of you that told him I was the killer."

All three of us looked at one another with downward-turned mouths and shook our heads. Each denied it, even though we knew it was me.

"And just so you know it, I had gotten a call from your good friend Perry Zella about coming to speak at his mystery group this afternoon. So my call log and Perry's call log proved it. I'd stepped out of the theater to take the call. When I came back in, Alan had already been killed."

His alibi seemed simple enough to check out, and I was sure he was right about Spencer looking into it.

"Are we done here?" Alan asked.

All three of us nodded.

"Maxine and Loretta, when the two of you are finished gossiping, I need to get some headshots for the review." He turned the knob and walked out the door.

"I guess he didn't do it. It just added up so good." Aunt Maxi patted me.

"That's the problem," Loretta griped. "All them crime shows make it out to be the obvious one as the main suspect, then boom!"

Aunt Maxi and I both jumped when Loretta yelled boom.

"The killer is no one you'd expect at all." She shrugged.

"This ain't no crime show. This here is real life, and if Mark didn't do it, it leaves Gretchen Cannon. And I'm going to get that fur coat from Perry Zella because it'll give me a chance to question Gretchen when I give it to her." I tapped my temple. "And I'll question Perry about Mark's alibi."

"Why would you do that if Spencer already checked it out?" Aunt Maxi asked and finished putting on the final touches of her makeup before the rehearsal's curtain call time.

"You never know." I didn't have an answer for her.

Maybe I needed to hear Mark's alibi from someone I trusted, like Perry. Or maybe it was curiosity to see if it did align with Perry's recollection of time.

Still... as a lawyer and now as a part-time sleuth, I left no stone unturned.

Going to the dry cleaners would be simple, since it was located right downtown. I even walked over there.

Perry's business was a simple little block building. The words Dry Cleaners were stenciled on the front window, and it was as simple as that. When you walked inside, the smell of the dry cleaning products hit you like a brick. There was a small counter in front of the guts of the cleaners.

Perry did his own laundering. He didn't send it out like most services.

"Hello, Roxy. I've got something so interesting to tell you." He pushed a button from underneath the counter, and the mechanical carousel with all the dry-cleaned clothes moved in a circular motion until Perry took his finger off the button.

"Yeah? I've got something to ask you." I watched him take the fur coat off the carousel.

"You first." He hung the heavy thing up on the metal hanger.

"Did you call Mark Redding yesterday morning?" I asked, not very sure of the time.

"Yeah. Actually, Spencer just left here after asking me the same thing. I even showed him my phone." He had the cleaning ticket in one hand and punched the register with the other hand. "I guess they are trying to cross suspects off their list of the murder of the producer."

"I'm guessing it all checked out?" I looked down at the screen and saw the total of the dry cleaning, which nearly knocked me off my feet.

"Sure did." He looked up and nodded towards the direction of the theater. "While we were talking, I heard all the sirens and then saw the ambulance. That's when he said he had to go because something was happening in the theater. Later he called me back to confirm him coming to the mystery meeting, and that's how I found out about the death."

"Crazy, right?" I tried to play off why I was asking and making it seem as if I was just curious, but it seemed Spencer was one leg ahead of me in this investigation.

"Here's something that's so crazy awesome I can't wait until our meeting tonight to tell the guys." He opened the fur coat and revealed a tag. "This is a true mystery right here. This was a real fur coat of Amanda B. Suculant."

"Is that someone from Honey Springs?" I asked with no idea who this person was.

"Are you kidding?" His eyes grew big and bright, his voice escalated. "Amanda B. Suculant was a true crime mystery. My club even read the unofficial autobiography. I really think this was her coat. She was murdered by her granddaughter. The granddaughter took off and went on the lam."

"I wonder how Gretchen got it." I looked a little closer at the tag.

"Amanda had all her coats made for her, and they all have these tags in them. Do you know how much one of her coats sold for at auction years ago?"

"No." I had no idea, but it was still an ugly coat.

"Over a million dollars. I can't believe it. I took so many photos of this so I could show my group." He was like a kid in a candy shop over this mystery. "They still never found the killer."

"I thought you said 'granddaughter'?" I asked and took the coat from him.

"They think it was the granddaughter, but they never found her." He held on to the coat, making me tug a little harder to get it from him. "I just wish I could take this to the meeting."

"Well, you can't. It's Gretchen's. Maybe she's the one who bought it for a million big ones." It made sense because she probably could afford it.

Plus, she would be the type to drop that kind of money down on something like this. Just in case it was this million-dollar coat, I told myself that I would lay it in the back seat of my car carefully when I got back to the theater, since I'd walked over to the dry cleaners.

When I shut the door, I noticed Butch Turner, the inspector who passed the theater, was walking into the Moose Lodge. There was no better time than the present to go over and check out the space for Emily's see-you-later party.

After all, it was my job to make sure the coffee was placed perfectly.

The Moose Lodge was a staple in practically every town in Kentucky. At any given time of the year, you'd find a wide array of activities to participate in both as an individual and as a family.

The events ranged from holiday parties, dances, sports, themed dinners, and live entertainment. There was a membership fee that let you use the lodge for those activities, but the bar was open to everyone in the community.

The bar was exactly where I found Butch, along with a pack of his cigarettes next to him.

"Howdy." I slid up next to Butch. "It's a little early for a drink."

"I know, I know why you're here." He reached over for the glass of water sitting in front of him. "And I'm not drinking. I'm meeting your husband here for an early lunch."

"Oh. Are you inspecting the building next to the Bean Hive, Mr. Inspector?" I teased and realized I couldn't've picked a worse time to have decided to come here.

Patrick.

"Code Enforcement Officer," Butch corrected me with his official title. "Yep. That's why we are meeting."

"I bet you don't know why I'm here." I leaned back on the bar, facing out into the space. "You obviously know, since you're meeting with Patrick, that Emily is closing the bakery and moving."

He gave a slight chin raise.

"Well, me and a few of our friends are giving her a see-you-later party here at the Moose, and I'd love for you to come." I pushed off the bar and nudged him. "I know you two have a fondness for each other, since you did give her a hard time about those pesky smoke detectors when she was building the bakery."

"We fought." He remembered. Dang.

"I wouldn't say you fought. I'd say you had very different views of the law." When I noticed he wasn't impressed with my interpretation of the event, I decided to just stroke his ego. "And you were right, just like you were with the Bean Hive."

"I better not come in there and see any sort of animal in that kitchen." He was oh-so charming.

"I think I'll put the coffee stand over there for the party." I pointed at the side wall and changed the subject. "I guess I better get going. I'm going to be heading on over to the theater because I have to drop off some coffee they've hired me to deliver."

It was my subtle segue to the real reason I was here.

"Speaking of the theater"—he met my words with a deep sigh—"I guess you heard about that sandbag falling on the producer."

"Mm-hhmm," he ho-hummed. "What are you beating around about?"

"Me? I was just making chitchat." I shrugged and kept my peripheral vision on the entrance in case Patrick came in.

"You know me enough. I'm not a chitchatter. You and I worked side by side a couple months before you opened, and we really worked in silence." He let out an even bigger sigh than before.

"I'm trying to figure out when you did the inspection last on the theater because the sheriff's department is pointing out something about the cord." I pretended that I didn't know the cord was cut.

Even though I didn't think Loretta was the killer, if she did come up and need my services, I was getting a jump on it. Though, technically, I'd get copies of the report if it came to that.

"I already turned everything in to Spencer." His words made my jaw drop. "You should know all about the last inspection because your husband had replaced the doors on the dressing rooms because the old ones weren't in good shape."

He jarred my memory of the Southern Women's Club fundraiser in which they needed to make repairs to the theater to keep it going, but I didn't recall Patrick saying his donation was because Butch had ordered the doors to be replaced.

"Dang. Spencer is ahead of me again," I muttered and decided it was high time to try to get into Spencer's brain to see exactly his next move.

"And he also knows that Loretta Bebe insisted on using the lowest grade cord possible to pass inspection. So I'm not saying the cord didn't deterio-rate with age, and I'm not saying someone didn't cut it." Butch was no help at all. "All I know is that it passed inspection, and I stand by my work."

"Well then." I clasped my hands in front of me and rocked back on my heels. "I hope we see you at the party tomorrow night."

"Tomorrow night." He gave a hard nod. "I just might show up for that coffee you're going to put right over there."

Did I mention how I was first in my class in the department of body language? Of course I did. I could tell by his body language that he'd already known I was there to pick his brain, not to look for a place for the coffee station.

"Yes. I think that's perfect." I squeezed my nose up and waved goodbye on my way out the door, thankful I didn't run into Patrick.

When I hurried across the street so Patrick didn't see me, I got into my car to text the group of girls before I gathered my thoughts about how I would ask Gretchen about the fur coat when I took it inside the theater.

My text to the group was about the space in the Moose and how it looked great as well as the perfect spot for the coffee. My text started the follow-up text, with everyone giving updates on their progress on their tasks for pulling off Emily's party. All of it was coming together, and everyone pulled their load, which was a blessing. I was fortunate to have such a great group of friends who were trustworthy, kind and all-around good people.

Checking to see if the internet was back was also a high priority. I wanted to Google Amanda B. Suculant and see if Gretchen did waste that much money on a fur coat.

I clicked on the internet icon and typed in Amanda B. Suculant only to be met with the rotating wheel of death. Meaning…the internet was still down.

The knock on the passenger-side window made me jump. Aunt Maxi was standing outside, laughing her head off.

"I just scared you to death," she mouthed and then pointed and continued to laugh. She opened the door and got in, putting her big hobo bag on the floor.

"What in earth is in there?" I asked.

"Things I need because I've gotten a bigger role." Aunt Maxi beamed with excitement. "At first I was worried about Loretta agreeing with Gretchen to let Sydney take control, but now that I've got a bigger role, I'm all good."

"What things do you need?" I glanced down at the bag, which overflowed with papers and tissues.

"I've got my makeup bag in there. Water. Spritzer for my skin." She patted her cheeks. "Plus notes on my performance." She shimmied her shoulders. "I had to do old-school acting in front of the mirror because I was going to watch some YouTube videos but that darn internet."

"It's ridiculous that we can't bring our town up to the technology to match the world." Suddenly I pictured Aunt Maxi in front of her mirror, making stabbing motions or whatever the mystery script had in it. I pinched my lips together so I didn't laugh at the image in my head. "Spencer said he was going to take up the internet issue with the town council because it's really hindered the investigation."

My phone chirped a text from Kayla.

Come anytime. I've already been to the mainland and back so I'm home all day.

"Who's that?" Aunt Maxi leaned over to see who was texting me. Her bag fell over, and she bent down and tried to shove everything back in her bag.

"Kayla. We are talking about the party for Emily. I hope you're coming."

"Crissy told me about it, and I plan on being there as long as we are out of rehearsal." Aunt Maxi hoisted the heavy hobo bag into her lap. "Speaking of rehearsal, I better get in there before we start."

"I have to take Gretchen her fancy coat." I pointed at the coat.

"How much do I owe you?" Aunt Maxi asked.

"Nothing." I didn't tell her the cost because it was ridiculous.

She opened the door.

"I'll be right in."

I waited until she was inside the building before I got out of my car and opened the back door to get the fur. But first I wanted to snap a photo of the label to be sure that when I did Google it, I had the correct spelling of the name.

I didn't want to go accusing anyone of anything if I didn't have all my T's crossed and I's dotted.

With the coat slung over my forearm, I headed into the theater and straight down the hallway to Gretchen's dressing room.

"Hi, Sydney."

Sydney was sitting in one of the chairs in Gretchen's dressing room, looking over what appeared to be the play's script.

"You got the coat back. That was quick." She smiled, stood up, and walked over to get it. "Gretchen will be thrilled." She leaned in and whispered, "Though she'd never tell you that."

"How's it going?" I asked with genuine concern.

"You know, since I saw you last night it's actually a little better. I went back up to the room, and Gretchen had made some great changes to the manuscript and really turned it into a nice play that I think will not only be well received by your community but even Broadway." She did seem much more relaxed. "In fact, she's doing an interview right now with Mark Redding. I haven't seen her do any press junkets for years. She offered Mark a job as her press secretary to get some gigs with different media outlets, since he knows so many people."

"Really?" I questioned.

"Yeah. Strange how she and Alan have spent so many years trying to boost each other's careers by all these favors when it was his death that really got the needle moving in her favor."

My heart skipped a beat. Did Sydney just give me another motive for Gretchen Cannon to be Alan Bogart's killer?

Sydney telling me how Gretchen's career had started to soar with the news of Alan's death only fueled my curiosity to see if she had any connection to the fur coat or the story of Amanda B. Suculant.

The only way to find out any answers in today's age was surfing the web, and last I checked, the internet was still down. But I was happy to see some work crews and big trucks working on some lines. I had no idea if those lines were for the internet, but I was putting all faith and hope that it was.

When I parked my car at the marina to have Big Bib boat me over to the Bee Farm, I noticed some papers on the floorboard of the passenger side where Aunt Maxi's hobo bag had dumped out. When I reached over to pick them up, I noticed it was her play's manuscript.

"Great," I said with a groan and looked up out of the windshield where Big Bib was looking back at me, waiting. I put the papers in my bag and decided they would have to wait until I got done with my business at the Bee Farm and then took the manuscript back to the theater.

Within minutes, with Big Bib's help and Bunny's willingness to stay at the Bean Hive for the whole day, I found myself back on Kayla's couch, enjoying another cup of her coffee while reading the fascinating story of Amanda B. Suculant and her life.

"She was a wealthy widow, and her husband was an oil man." I didn't read in too much detail about that. "It says here she was a big supporter of the arts."

I grabbed my bag and took out Aunt Maxi's play manuscript to grab the notebook I'd put in there. I wanted to take notes on the article, since Kayla had forgotten to get copy paper when she did boat over to Honey Springs.

"Gretchen," Kayla said, gasping.

"And look." I pointed at a photo I'd found of Gretchen and Amanda together at a big charity event. "If they weren't friends, they knew each other."

"According to the article, Amanda was found dead in the freezer in the garage." I didn't want to picture it.

"Chopped up?" Kayla made a crunched-up face and dragged Aunt Maxi's manuscript off the coffee table. She sat back and started to thumb through it.

"No. All in one piece like her killer cared about her and really tried to preserve the body or something. I'd read a case once where someone had been murdered by a family member and put them in a stand-up freezer at their family restaurant in a brown sack that others thought was frozen meat." I vaguely remembered the case, but it was the conclusion that stuck in my head. "The family member who killed subconsciously wanted to be found out and did want the body to be preserved so they could eventually have a funeral. I bet it was the same with Amanda. That's why they think it's the granddaughter that killed her."

"It makes sense. But what does this have to do with Gretchen?" she asked.

"That's a good question." I picked up my phone and showed her the photo of the label I'd taken of the fur coat. "According to everything I've found so far on here, Amanda's coats were auctioned off, and there are photos of them. Nowhere did I find this coat. I'm not saying it couldn't have been sold outside of auction. So I'm not sure. It just seems odd this dead woman's coat is on Gretchen and now the producer is dead."

"Roxy!" Kayla gasped and jumped up, waving Aunt Maxi's manuscript in the air. "I think we have our answer." She shoved the pack of papers in my face. "Have you read this?"

"No. Aunt Maxi said it's great and is excited about it. Why?" I put the laptop on the coffee table and stood up next to Kayla to look at what she was overly excited about.

"This play reads a lot like Amanda B. Suculant's life, only the names have been changed." She handed me the manuscript.

"What?" I looked down at the papers in my hand while Kayla pointed out the various similar accounts that we were reading on the internet.

"I'll get us another cup of coffee while you read that."

My head was in a tailspin as I scanned more of the manuscript. The similarities were uncanny.

"I'll get that coffee later." I quickly texted Big Bib and asked if he could come get me. I knew it wouldn't take him long since the temperature was up, the snowstorm had long passed, and the ice on the lake was melting. "I need to get Aunt Maxi out of that theater."

"It does all add up. Gretchen came here cashing in on her favor. She and Alan had all those fights." Kayla blinked several times, recounting all the things I'd told her. "But don't you think it's dangerous for you to go in there? Don't you think you should call Spencer?"

"I want to get Aunt Maxi out of there, then I'll call Spencer." I gathered all my things, shoved them into my bag, and walked out the door. Down the path I went.

CHAPTER SEVENTEEN

*N*ot that I wasn't grateful the crew was working on the lines, but it was just annoying how they'd stopped traffic while I finished up one of the wires. Traffic wasn't bad—it was only one other car and me—but there I sat. In my car. Stopped. Annoyed.

"Hi." I had rolled down my window and called out to the lady with the stop sign.

She walked over.

"Is this going to take long?" I asked.

"No. We just need to get the bucket down so we can move over to the last box and get the internet up and running." She was pleasant, even though she shivered from the cold.

"Great. How long do you think it'll be?" I asked.

"Before you can go or the internet comes up?" She wanted clarification.

"Both?" I asked with a smile in hopes I wasn't annoying her.

"Looks like you're about to go now and in about an hour for the internet." She flipped the stop sign to the other side and motioned for me to go.

When I got to the theater, Aunt Maxi was on stage with Gretchen, who was directing her. She was totally into her part. Aunt Maxi was playing who I considered to be the character equivalent to Amanda B. Suculant, and Crissy appeared to be playing the relative. I stood there with my eye on Gretchen.

Aunt Maxi didn't appear to be in immediate danger, so the more nonchalant I was, the better.

The play seemed to take a turn in the middle. When I read it, it appeared that the ghost of Amanda B. Suculant haunted the family member who killed her, so it wasn't exactly how the true crime went but close enough to get my attention. None other than Gretchen played the ghost.

While they played out the scene, I continued to type in the Google search on my phone to see if the internet was back up. I knew the lady had told me about an hour, but I could pray it would be earlier.

"Granddaughter of Amanda B. Suculant," I said out loud and typed into the search engine.

"Cut!" Sydney's voice boomed over the actors. "I don't think the lighting is right. George, do you think you could lay off the purple tone and do a simple sunrise blue?"

George, who I assumed was one of the crew's lighting guys, waved a hand and started to push all sorts of buttons on the control panel from his area in the back of the theater where all that stuff was kept.

"Take five!" Sydney held her hand up in the air. "Good work, people."

From the way the actors were smiling, I could tell Sydney's directing was a far cry from how Alan had handled them.

I couldn't help but watch Gretchen leave the stage. I got up to follow her out into the hall, where I bet she was going to her dressing room. When I peeked inside, she wasn't there, but the briefcase was on the table.

Alan's briefcase. The one I'd seen him with when I walked in on him when he was in here reading his manuscript.

"Hey there." Sydney walked up behind me. "What's going on?"

"I was looking for my aunt Maxi. She left her script in my car." I pulled it out of my bag and followed Sydney into the dressing room.

"She must've memorized it because she's doing great. She's a natural." Sydney sat down with her papers in her hand and pulled the pencil from behind her ear. "Dang. Tip is broken off." She looked in the briefcase, shuffling through before she found another pencil.

"Is that yours?" I asked about the briefcase.

"Yeah. I got it back in film school." She sat down and started to mark on the paper.

The sound of dings came from my phone and her phone, then vague, distant sounds of dings went off down the hall. A few woohoos could be heard in the distance.

"I think we just got internet. That would be great!" Sydney was so excited.

I pulled my phone out, wondering if I was standing there with the real killer. While I pretended to be paying attention to my phone, various things started to pop into my head that would actually make sense if Sydney did kill Alan Bogart.

When I looked at the internet on my phone, my search engine popped up the last thing I'd Googled, Amanda B. Suculant's granddaughter. A photo of a young woman with brown hair popped up. I looked up at Sydney and tried to picture her with brown hair that was not the deep brown.

She looked at me and smiled.

"The internet is a good thing." She went back to her phone.

I looked back and forth a few times between the photo on my phone and her. The granddaughter's name was Carrow Suculant. The girl in the photo didn't seem as meek and quiet as the woman sitting in front of me.

"Are you okay, Roxy?" she asked when she looked up and I was just staring at her with a blank face.

"Why?" I knew it was her when I noticed the eyes were the same. "Why did you kill your grandmother?"

"What?" She laughed.

"This." I wagged Aunt Maxi's copy of the manuscript. "You killed your grandmother. You knew Gretchen from the arts where your

145

grandmother took you. I'm not sure how you got to working for Gretchen, but somehow you went to college for film then wrote this transcript where you detailed the crime you committed but tweaked it enough with the ghost to throw people off."

She started to laugh. Her attitude only fueled me more.

"The other morning when I was delivering the coffee and the romance play was still the production, I was dropping off Gretchen's personal requests, and I found Alan in here. I thought he was looking at his briefcase, but he found your life story in there. This." I wagged the papers even harder when I recognized her facial features had turned a little sterner. I knew I was on the right track. "When you found out Alan had stolen your manuscript, you killed him. I honestly thought it was Gretchen after I picked up the fur from the cleaners and Perry told me about the tag and the history of your grandmother. I couldn't understand why Gretchen had the fur, but now I know it's a prop. A prop in your sick manuscript."

"Aren't you just the nosiest citizen in this little town?" Sydney's head tilted. "You know nothing about my life."

"Oh. I think I'm right. Look at you. You're shaking, you're so nervous." I pointed out how the papers in her hand were shaking.

"I'm fine." She put the papers in the open briefcase but still held the pencil in her grip. Her hands fisted. "You just don't understand. This business is cutthroat. Alan stole from me."

"You thought writing the manuscript was going to clear your conscience of killing your grandmother?" I started to pepper her with questions to try to confuse her more and buy me time to come up with a way to get the heck out of there.

"She cut me out of her will," Sydney seethed and lunged towards me with the pencil above her head.

I smacked her arm out of the way and fell to the side.

"There's no way you're going to get out of here alive." Her eyes were on fire. She shut the door of the dressing room and locked it.

"Help!" I screamed.

"These doors are soundproof, like most doors in theater dressing rooms, so actors can rehearse lines." She thought she was so clever, but she didn't know Honey Springs dressing rooms. They were not anything special. Like Butch had said earlier, Patrick had donated the doors from a pile he had left over from another job at Cane Construction, and they weren't fancy, noise-proof doors.

"Help!" I continued to scream as she got closer.

I swung my bag at her as she shifted from side to side. Each time she got a little closer, she swung her arm down, trying to stab me with the pencil. I knew I couldn't die from a pencil, but it might stop me from getting away from her.

I kept one eye on her and one eye on the path to the door, only she continued to hop around like a little jumping bean.

"You think you can turn me in? Now that I have reached a level of fame in my career and no longer need to be under the control of Gretchen Cannon?" She came at me a couple of additional times.

"Help!" I continued to scream, hoping anyone would be walking past the door and hear me.

A thud and splintering wood shard flying in the air made Sydney and me turn to the door.

"Hold it right there." Spencer Shepard was staring down the barrel of his gun, which was pointed directly at Sydney O'Neal.

CHAPTER EIGHTEEN

"*T*ell us one more time how you figured it out?"

I stood in the middle of the coffee shop, telling Perry Zella and his mystery group all the details of how I'd figured out that Alan's killer was Sydney, also known as Carrow Suculant, the granddaughter of Amanda B. Suculant.

On the night of Sydney and Gretchen's arrest, Perry still held the mystery club meeting at the coffee shop, and I was all too happy to tell them about it.

"After Kayla had read the manuscript while I was looking up Amanda, she said it was eerily like Amanda's life. I remembered seeing Alan in Gretchen's dressing room with the briefcase. He'd found the manuscript and took it for the play." Of course I had hand gestures and facial features to go along with my story to make it a lot more interesting.

I continued.

"When the internet pinged on my phone, it was then that it brought up my last search, which was the photo of Carrow. I recognized by the eyes it was Sydney and that it was her briefcase Alan had taken the new play from. It was hers. She had written it as a way of letting out her feelings about killing her grandmother."

"It was her sick way of making herself feel less guilty," Perry said and looked around at his club. "This has happened in crimes before. The killer needs closure for themselves."

"Right." Mark Redding chimed in and continued to write in his little notebook.

"I wasn't sure how Gretchen fit in, but according to Spencer, she somehow figured out Sydney was the killer, and she blackmailed her into working for her. Even taking one of Amanda's fur coats in exchange for helping Carrow change her identity." It was crazy how it all turned out, and I was still trying to wrap my head around it and the danger everyone was in. "Gretchen and Sydney knew Alan had stolen the manuscript from the briefcase, so they hatched a plan for them to create a big argument. While Gretchen made a scene, Sydney slipped off stage. She knew all about the ins and outs of the theater, since it was her degree, and she knew if she cut the rope, the sandbag would kill Alan."

"So she did take the ax from Newton's wheelbarrow?" Perry asked.

"She did. When they saw Newton's tools, they'd devised a plan the night before in their hotel room to carry out the plan." It was crazy how many details Gretchen had put into it. "Gretchen was the mastermind that fed Sydney's guilt. Gretchen also thought that she could get out of being under arrest for murder since she didn't actually cut the rope, but that's not how it's going to go down."

"This is crazy." Perry shook his head. "And to think a big murder like Amanda B. Suculant from years ago would be solved in small town Honey Springs."

The days following the big arrests were kind of crazy. Gretchen and Sydney had been transported to a federal prison while they went through the legal process. I'd given my statement. Loretta had changed the play back to the sweet romance, and everyone was happy with their parts and the simplicity of just entertaining the citizens of Honey Springs.

It did take a few trips and the community coming together to switch out the props, but in the end, it all worked out.

Even Emily's see-you-later party was fabulous. It was a big time, and she was thrilled to see all the people coming together.

Though I was happy for her moving and getting on with her life, I was even more excited about what was happening today.

"I can't believe this is happening." I reached over to Patrick, who was sitting in the chair beside me in front of Evan Rich's desk at the Honey Springs National Bank. I squeezed Patrick's hand.

Evan was busy eating a couple of the pecan balls and sipping the coffee I'd brought him. He watched the printer spit out the papers needed for me to sign to make the Queen for the Day building, which was next to the Bean Hive, all mine.

Tamara had already purchased Bees Knees Bakery right after Emily moved away from Honey Springs.

"I'm excited about the roastery. I think it'll be a cool addition to our town." Evan slid the papers across his desk in front of me and put a pen on top. "As soon as you sign the loan papers, I'll get the necessary paperwork over to Penney, and she'll finish the closing."

"Sounds good." I couldn't stop smiling.

"Speaking of Penney, how is she?" Evan asked about my mom, who was the local real estate agent.

"She's doing great. In fact, she has been on a vacation, and Patrick and I are meeting her at her office after we leave here so we can discuss all the crazy things that took place while she was gone." I signed on the line and pushed the papers back to him. "How is Emily doing?"

"She's settling in. And Mocha." He shook his bald head and smiled. "Emily loves that cat."

"Great. I'm so glad it worked out for both of them." When Emily had come into the Bean Hive to give me her final goodbye, she couldn't leave without adopting Mocha. The match was purr-fect for them both.

"Well, congratulations." Evan, Patrick, and I stood up. Evan shook our hands. "It looks like you're going to be busy with construction the next few months."

"Good." Patrick spoke up. "Anything to keep her mind occupied with something other than murder investigations."

Evan was right. I was going to be busy the next couple of months getting the building ready for the new roastery and maintaining my tour schedule, but if another murder investigation came up, I was not so sure the roastery would occupy me that much.

What was Patrick thinking? I thought with a simple smile on my face.

The End

Keep reading for a sneak peek of the next book in the series. Frothy Foul Play is now available to purchase on Amazon.

Chapter One of Book Nine
Frothy Foul Play

Morning was always my favorite part of the day. Maybe it was the feeling of a fresh start. Maybe it was the amazing sunrise that lit up the sky with glorious oranges and reds that skidded across the calm water off Lake Honey Springs. Or just maybe it was the smell of the freshly brewed coffee that filtered throughout the Bean Hive, my coffee shop.

I sighed as I shifted my gaze away from the boardwalk and peered over my shoulder at the clock on the wall behind the counter.

Soon, my only employee would be walking through the door, and shortly after that, she'd be followed by our first customer of the day.

I was very appreciative of my customers, but the sound of Pepper, my schnauzer, snoring lightly, all snuggled up in his bed next to the fireplace, sparked a joy deep in my heart.

With a mug of hot coffee nestled between my hands, I turned my eyes back on the sunrise, inhaling a deep breath to get the most aromatic whiff possible of my cup of wake-me-up, and then closed my eyes. I felt the first warm rays of sun reach down the pier and across the boardwalk and kiss my face.

"Welcome, sun," I whispered and opened my eyes, pushing my black curly hair behind my shoulders.

I set my cup down, firmly planted my elbows on the long bar that ran across the front of the entire coffee shop, and rested my chin in my hands as I reflected on what the day ahead was going to look like.

With all this Zen talk from Crissy Lane about her new Bee Happy Resort adventure, I thought she might be converting me over to the quiet life.

Drip, drip, drip.

The sound of the industrial coffee makers working was music to my ears. The smell of the freshly roasted beans I'd created in my own roastery blanketed the coffee shop, lending warm and cozy comfort to what was a cool morning.

With what few moments I had left to myself before the hustle and bustle, I closed my eyes again. I couldn't stop myself from smiling when I thought about Crissy Lane. She told me that if I outwardly smiled, then I'd smile inwardly too. She was right. Or it was the coffee. Either way, I was willing to give her the credit.

Knock, knock, knock.

I opened one eye to see who on earth was tapping on the picture window in front of me.

There was no denying that the big-haired shadow standing right in the way of the morning sunrise was in fact my aunt, Maxine Bloom.

"Whatcha doing in there?" she mouthed through the glass before pointing with her free hand to the door, motioning for me to open up while using her other hand to steady her bike, which she refused to put in the bike rack on the edge of the boardwalk.

Instead, she propped it up against the front of the coffee shop and jerked her hobo bag out of the wire basket strapped to the front.

Pepper heard her and came running to the door, wagging his little tail in anticipation of the treat he knew Aunt Maxi had for him.

Aunt Maxi bolted into the door once I unlocked it. "I said, 'What are you doing with your eyes closed?' Are you tired? Are you and Patrick having problems?" She gasped, dropping her bag to the ground and throwing her hands over her mouth. "Oh my gawd! You're pregnant!"

"No. No. And no!" That last "no" definitely ended in an exclamation point. Not that I didn't want children, but Patrick Cane and I hadn't been married too terribly long, and we still just wanted to enjoy our time together. "The only kids I've got are Pepper and Sassy."

I picked up her bag, shooing Pepper from it, and handed it to her.

Aunt Maxi cocked her head to the side and shook the bag before resigning to the little silver-and-white dog begging at her feet.

"I reckon you do have these little babies." She wagged her finger, gesturing for me to open her bag. Once I did, she reached in and pulled out a plastic baggie with the Walk in the Bark logo printed on the front and tasty homemade dog treats inside. "Where's Sassy?" she asked, looking around for the black standard poodle that I'd gotten with the marriage.

"Patrick took her to work with him today. He's got a few things to finish at the Bee Happy Resort before Crissy's big weekend. Sassy loves running around the island while he works there." The sun's rays had finally made their way across the entire shop, giving it an inviting glow.

"New hair color?" I asked when I noticed the bright-yellow color and purple streaks in her hair.

"I like it." She raked her hand upward through her hair. "It's bright and cheery."

"It is that." I gave her a hug. I loved how she was her own person and never cared what others thought about her ever-changing hair colors. "I'm guessing Crissy's new replacement did that?" I asked after I gave her another quick hug.

Aunt Maxi only pulled out a can of hair spray from her bag.

"Oh no. Don't you be spraying that in here," I told her and reached around to flip the Closed sign on the door to Open, even though it technically wasn't opening time.

Did she ever listen to me? Nope.

She pressed her finger on the aerosol cans nozzle and sprayed it at full strength all over her head, missing most of her hair.

"Pft, pft." I spat and waved my hand in front of my face as I passed her on my way to the back of the coffeehouse.

There was no time to dillydally. I had to get the rest of the coffee shop ready to open, and that meant the opening ritual.

"Stop spraying that stuff in here. It might get on the food," I said as I went over my mental checklist of tasks like refilling the coffee-bar condiments and the tea bar.

"It's no different than dog hair or cat hair or whatever else Louise Carlton will be bringing in today." She shrugged and put the can back in her bag as she weaved in and out of the tables on her way back to the counter.

"I don't know what animal Louise is bringing in this morning, but I'm excited to give the baby a fur-ever home." I delighted in the fact that

I had a small hand in giving the homeless animals in Honey Springs a warm and loving home.

There was no doubt that I'd jumped through a lot of hoops to get the health department to even approve the collaboration I had with Pet Palace. It was what some towns called the SPCA, but since Honey Springs was a small Kentucky town, there weren't any sort of funds for a local SPCA. That's when Louise Carlton had opened the nonprofit no-kill shelter, where I volunteered once a week like most of us around here.

In fact, I'd had a terrible case of loneliness when I moved to Honey Springs permanently and opened the coffeehouse upon being nudged by Aunt Maxi. I'd met Louise when she came in to get a cup of coffee, and she'd told me she had the cure for my lonely nights. That cure was Pepper.

I knew I had to help other little furry animals find homes, so each week, I began featuring one of the Pet Palace animals at the coffeehouse, and we'd had a one hundred percent adoption streak.

"Did you know all the rooms at the Cocoon Hotel are booked?" Aunt Maxi made small talk while I checked on the status of the coffeepots, which were in full percolating mode.

I nodded and got out the container of creamer to fill up the little ceramic cows on all of the café tables that dotted the inside of the coffeehouse. "That's a good thing for Crissy. I'm excited for her."

"I'm gonna help you so that I can sit with my niece for a good cup of coffee this morning." Aunt Maxi looked back at the door. "Where is your employee, anyways?"

She hung her purse on the coatrack next to the counter in exchange for one of the Bean Hive aprons I required the employees to wear while they were working.

Aunt Maxi looked around and immediately started to work on the checklist for opening the coffee shop.

I loved that about her. Even though she didn't work here, she always wanted what was best for me and helped me whenever she could. Plus, she had never been one of those people who was good at idly sitting around while things needed to be accomplished. She was one of those people who could just pick up a task before being told to do it. She had an eye for seeing what needed to be done and doing it.

"Thank you for helping me." I loved her so much. She was the reason I'd come to stay here every summer and the reason I lived here now. "I'm sure Bunny will be here any minute."

"Why aren't these youngins doing all of this at closing?" Aunt Maxi huffed even though she loved when I praised her. She made her way over to the far end of the L-shaped counter, where the tea bar was located.

"Hmm. Let me see." Aunt Maxi reviewed the station to see what needed to be done. She moved various packets of tea and opened the base cabinets to get more single-serves and refill the loose tea containers of stir sticks, sweeteners, and condiments like honey.

"It's hard to find good help nowadays," I said and made sure the centerpieces on each café table were properly placed.

When I'd opened the Bean Hive, I knew it had an atmosphere that was warm and inviting. The coffee was just a bonus, along with the cozy community.

"Hi, do," Bunny Bowowski trilled when she shuffled through the door, letting the cold air rush in behind her.

"Speak of the devil," Aunt Maxi said under her breath and brushed the edge of the apron along the top of the tea bar before she headed to the opposite side of the counter to tidy up the coffee self-serve bar.

"What on earth does that mean, Maxine Bloom?" Bunny gave Aunt Maxi a hard stare as she pulled from her hair the pins that were holding her pillbox hat in place. It was no secret they weren't the best of friends, and Aunt Maxi was good at poking the bear.

"Roxy was saying how it was hard to get good help, and well"—Aunt Maxi shrugged—"you walked in."

"Oh, stop it. I wasn't talking about you." I rushed over to help Bunny with her things. She was elderly and slow, but she was good at making customers feel welcome. Plus, she needed something to do during the days, so when she'd asked for a job, I was delighted to have her.

"We were talking about the afternoon kids completing the checklist, like restocking the coffee and tea bar." I put the creamer container on the table and gave Aunt Maxi a little bow. "Which I'm grateful Aunt Maxi is doing for us."

"Doing for Roxanne." Aunt Maxi made it clear she wasn't doing Bunny any favors.

"I don't know what I'd do if you two ever got along," I teased as I placed Bunny's handbag underneath the counter and headed back through the swinging door to the kitchen, where I needed to get another container of creamer to have on hand at the counter and check on the sweet treats in the oven.

I wasn't back there for too long by myself because Bunny, Aunt Maxi, and Pepper had followed me. Aunt Maxi planted herself on the stool that butted up to the metal workstation where I did all the preparing for the cooking and baking.

Aunt Maxi licked her lips when she noticed the donuts I'd taken out of the fryer earlier this morning and placed on the cooling rack so I could get them iced and displayed before the first customer of the day. "I love a good donut."

"Your favorite too." I opened the oven door to check on the muffins then set the timers for a smidgen longer since I noticed they weren't quite done.

The other oven had the breakfast quiches, and they were still a little jiggly in the middle, so I upped the time on those too.

"We need to keep an eye on the quiches," I told Bunny on my way over to the walk-in refrigerator to get the container of creamer.

"Strawberry and cream?" Aunt Maxi's eyes grew, and she licked her lips like she could taste them.

"Those aren't for you," Bunny told Aunt Maxi in a sharp voice. "Let me get you a coffee." Bunny made her way over to my small coffeepot that I kept in the kitchen for us and made herself, as well as Aunt Maxi, a cup of coffee.

"Mm-hmm," I said and bent down to grab the creamer from the refrigerator. "And the donuts are for book club tonight, so none this morning." I put the creamer next to her on the workstation so she could doctor up her coffee.

"All of those can't be for book club." Aunt Maxi leaned a little to the left to look around me at the cooling rack of all the donuts. "One little, tiny one?" She used her thumb and pointer finger to show me just how tiny she meant, with her eye looking through the space between them.

"Nope." I stopped and took a treat from Pepper's treat jar since he was so cute sitting next to Aunt Maxi, hoping she would get a donut and accidentally drop a morsel for him. "You haven't told me why you're out so early this morning."

The bell above the door in the coffeehouse dinged, and we all looked at one another. I nodded over to the muffins, cookies, and bagels I'd already gotten on the display trays.

"Everyone grab a tray. We've got an early one." I walked through the swinging kitchen door with the creamer in one hand and a glass pie plate holding a blueberry tart in the other. Aunt Maxi and Bunny both followed me with their hands full.

"Good morning," I called out to our first customer of the day, who was next to the self-serve, pay-by-good-faith coffee bar. "I've got the coffee coming right up. Just got finished brewing."

I put the creamer on the counter along with the tart, and then Bunny's eyes met mine, and she knew what I was thinking. She began to put all the treats in the display cases, write their names on the small chalkboards on the front, and write all the specials on one of the big chalkboards on the wall while I continued to put the coffee carafes on the coffee bar.

The Bean Hive was located in the middle of the boardwalk, right across from the pier and was a perfect stop for anyone who worked in downtown Honey Springs or even just the tourists who came to visit our little town.

I was very proud of how I'd transformed the old building and kept the exposed brick walls and wooden ceiling beams in their original form.

With some elbow grease—and binge-watching DIY videos on

YouTube to figure out how to make the necessary repairs to pass inspection—the Bean Hive had become a great success over the years, and the friendships I'd built had become priceless.

"To answer your question from a few minutes ago—I dropped by to ask if you were going to book club and wanted to pick me up tonight," Aunt Maxi said.

"Yes, I'm going, and yes, I'll pick you up." Not that I was planning on leaving the coffeehouse today, since the book club was at the Crooked Cat, the bookstore at the end of the boardwalk.

I was involved in a lot of committees in Honey Springs, and some days, it was just easier to stay at the coffeehouse all day instead of driving to my house, which was really only a seven-minute drive. Plus, there was always something to do here.

"Is there anything else we can get you?" I asked the customer and received a shake of his head before he dropped his dollars in the good-faith jar. "We have some delicious cream cheese–topped carrot-and-raisin muffins that pair well with our in-house New Year Blend I noticed you got."

"No. I'm sure I'll be coming back for some more later this week." He sounded pretty confident, and that made me curious as to why he was in Honey Springs, since I didn't recognize him—which told me he was a tourist.

"Are you here for pleasure or business?"

He turned around when I asked him the question and unzipped his coat as he surveyed the coffee shop.

"I guess you could say both." He offered a smile.

I looked into his black eyes to see what kind of man my customer was and whether or not I could read his personality from his body language.

"My wife begged me to come and do an article on the new health and wellness spa. Honey Happy or…" He trailed off as he tried to recall the right name. "We just pulled into town and are about to get our room."

"Bee Happy Resort?" Excitement filled every part of me, knowing how much work Crissy had put into her new retreat resort over the past nine or ten months.

"Yes, for the retreat, but we aren't staying at the resort itself," he said with a stiff voice. He rolled his hand in the air, with a stir stick between his fingers. "Anyways, my wife likes all the holistic stuff, and I write for *Healthy Women's Magazine*." He looked around. "In fact, I just might like to do an article on this little gem." He smiled again, and this time, his dimples deepened above the beard.

"Really?" This seemed like a nice opportunity for me and one I didn't want to pass up. "I'd love for you to." I hurried over to the counter and plucked a tissue from the box. "Let me get you some strawberry-and-cream donuts to take back to your wife as well as one of the carrot muffins."

"I wouldn't want to…" He was going to try to stop me, but I wasn't going to let that happen.

"I insist." I actually put two muffins in the box. "I think you're going to fall in love with our welcoming community while your wife is enjoying her time at the Bee Happy Resort."

The door of the coffeehouse opened.

Crissy Lane walked in, and with the sun up over the trees, the rays sprinkled in and cast yellow highlights on Crissy's sun-washed blond hair, which wasn't at all as natural as she proclaimed.

"Speaking of Bee Happy Resort." I turned his attention to Crissy as I waved her over. "This is the owner, Crissy Lane."

"Crissy, this is—" I turned to my customer. "I'm sorry. I didn't get your name."

"Tom Foster." He took the box of treats from me.

"Crissy, Tom and his wife are here for the opening of Bee Happy Resort." This was great because that meant there were two people going to her grand opening weekend.

The reservations for the weekend retreat had been slow when she'd opened them up a couple of months ago and had started her marketing campaign to push for clients. She'd been driving all of her friends crazy about coming because she needed warm bodies to fill the camera space since she'd sent out all the media releases with free treatments for the first five reporters and social media influencers to sign up.

"It's so nice to meet you early." Crissy smiled, batting her long, fake eyelashes at him.

Pretty much everything on her was fake, down to her ta-tas. She had a heart of gold and truly did love all things spa. Since she was already a nail technician as well as a hairdresser, opening a resort was in her wheelhouse, and she was good at it.

However, I did love her natural red hair over her box-dye job. She had the cutest red freckles along her cheeks that made an adorable bridge across her nose and were the same shade as her real hair color, but she tried to cover those, too, with all sorts of makeup.

"He's with *Healthy Women's Magazine*." I bounced on my toes at the thought of him actually doing an article on the Bean Hive.

"Then we have to sit down, and you can let me show you the ins and outs of the spa. I think your readers are going to love it." She curled her hand into the crook of his elbow, her long nails capturing the fabric of his shirt like a cat clawing its prey. "I insist on giving your wife a free facial that she'll never forget." Crissy's twangy voice dripped with Southern charm as she steered him away from the coffee bar. "Where are y'all staying?"

"The Cocoon," I overheard him tell Crissy. I smiled since it was so good Crissy's new endeavor was bringing in business for Camey Montgomery, the owner of the Cocoon Hotel. And Tom was probably on the boardwalk this morning taking a stroll when he just so happened upon the Bean Hive for a great cup of coffee, if I did say so myself.

"What's all the nonsense about?" Aunt Maxi asked, both of us watching as Crissy took him over to the couch next to the fireplace and helped prop his back up with a few of the pillows.

"Crissy being Crissy." I laughed and turned back to Aunt Maxi. "I'll pick you up around five for book club."

"Mm-hmm. Did you tell her?" Aunt Maxi threw a glance over at Crissy.

"No." I shook my head and knew that after her little meeting with

Tom, I had to tell her I didn't have anyone to work at the Bean Hive for the weekend, so I wasn't going to be able to go to her grand opening. "But I will."

"I don't envy you." Aunt Maxi patted me on the arm. "Anyways, I've got to get going." She grabbed her hobo bag from the coat-tree and pulled it across her body. She put her hand in the bag and pulled out a small thermos. "I've got to meet an Airbnb client in about ten minutes, so I wanted to grab a couple of donuts and a cup of coffee to take." She unscrewed the lid and put the thermos under the coffee carafe, filling it up.

"You are brilliant." I couldn't help but smile at her coming here to get my coffee to entice her new tenants. "Make sure you leave a Bean Hive business card next to the goodies. I'll be sure to bring you a couple strawberry-and-cream ones at the book club." I buttoned the top button of her coat for her. "Make sure you bundle up. I have no idea why you rode your bike, anyways. It's still not spring, and it's cold."

"I'll be fine. I'll see you at 5:00 p.m. sharp." She gave me a long, level look that reminded me of how she liked to be on time.

Honey Springs was such a small community that every business was pretty much independently owned, and we relied on each other to promote and support our businesses. That's why I used the Bee Farm's honey in all of my recipes that called for honey, kept the information for the Cocoon Hotel at the counter, and promoted adoptions for Pet Palace, among many other things.

"I'll be there," I assured her but didn't commit to an exact time in fear I wouldn't be able to close on time since I didn't have any help this afternoon.

I walked her to the door and watched her secure the thermos and to-go box of donuts in her wire basket before she tried to pedal off, nearly running over Louise Carlton in the process.

"Bunny," I called over my shoulder when I saw Louise Carlton say something to Aunt Maxi before Aunt Maxi left in the direction of the Cocoon Hotel. "Do you mind changing the menus? Louise is here, and it looks like she's got a cat in the carrier."

"I reckon I can." Bunny tried not to show how much she really did like to draw on the chalkboard menus that I'd opted for instead of paper menus.

When I originally opened the Bean Hive, I had attached the chalkboard menus to the wall, which forced me to either take them down or stand on a stool to write on them. Patrick decided he'd had enough of worrying about me falling off the stool, so he created a pully system that allowed us to move the boards up and down with a chain, making it easier for Bunny to take over that job.

"The specials are written on the piece of paper next to the register," I told her and headed over to the door to let Louise in since her hands were full. "Don't forget to add the cream cheese-topped carrot-and-raisin muffins."

It was a new recipe that I had given great consideration when I'd made the New Year Blend at my roastery. I wanted to create a menu that married the food with the coffee choices. Since we weren't open on Sundays, I spent most of those afternoons testing and trying out various combinations to come up with just the right pairing. I was very proud of this new muffin-and-coffee combination.

"Good morning!" Louise's smile was as bright at the morning sun. Her eyes lit up underneath her bangs as the sun bounced off the silver bob that made her look so sophisticated. "You aren't going to believe this little beauty."

She held up the cage of the cutest smoosh-faced black kitten.

"Achoo!" The loudest sneeze came from Tom Foster, making me jump all the way to heaven.

"Good night!" Bunny hollered, throwing her hands up to her chest. "You almost made me pee myself."

"Is-is-is…" He stood up from the couch where Crissy had had him pinned, his nose curled and his eyes squinted. "Is that a—achoo!" He snorted. "A cat?"

Frothy Foul Play is now available to purchase on Amazon.

RECIPES FROM THE BEAN HIVE

Pecan Balls
Salmon Cat Treats
Coffee Soufflé
Maple Pecan Breakfast Ring

Pecan Balls

Submitted by Gayle Shanahan

Ingredients

- 1 stick butter, softened
- 2 T sugar
- 1 C flour
- 1 t vanilla
- 1 C ground pecans
- Powdered sugar

Directions

1. Mix all ingredients, except powdered sugar, well.
2. Form into small balls.
3. Bake 15 minutes at 325°.
4. While still warm, roll cookies into powdered sugar.

Enjoy!

Salmon Cat Treats

Ingredients

- Can Salmon
- One Egg
- ½ cup flour

Directions

1. Pulse the canned salmon in a food processor and chop finely.
2. Combine salmon, egg, and flour in stand-up mixer until it forms a dough.
3. Roll out dough to 1/4 inch thickness on a floured surface.
4. Use a cookie cutter (I recommend a 3/4 inch cutter) to cut into pieces.
5. Put the treats on a baking sheet and bake at 350°F for 20 minutes.

Coffee Soufflé

Submitted by Andrea Stoeckel

Ingredients

- 1 envelope (1 tablespoon) unflavored gelatin
- 1 1/2 cups brewed coffee, cooled
- 1/2 cup milk
- 1/2 cup white sugar, divided
- 1/4 teaspoon salt, divided
- 3 eggs, separated
- 1/2 teaspoon vanilla extract

Directions

1. Combine gelatin and cold coffee in a small bowl; set aside for 5 minutes to soften.
2. In a heat-proof bowl or the top of a double boiler, combine coffee mixture, milk, 1/4 cup sugar, 1/8 teaspoon salt, and the egg yolks.
3. Set the bowl over a pan of simmering water.
4. Stir until sugar is dissolved and gelatin has melted.
5. Whisk in remaining 1/4 cup sugar, 1/8 teaspoon salt, and the egg yolks.
6. Cook and stir until mixture is thick and creamy and coats the back of a metal spoon.
7. Remove from heat.
8. Whip the egg whites (with a pinch of salt, if desired) until stiff peaks form.
9. Fold egg whites and vanilla into slightly cooled custard.
10. Pour into a serving dish or lightly greased mold.
11. Chill until set, at least 4 hours.

Maple Pecan Breakfast Ring

Ingredients

- 1 cup milk
- 1/2 stick butter (1/4 cup)
- 1/4 cup sugar
- 1/4 cup softened butter
- 1/2 cup finely chopped pecans
- 1/4 cup sugar
- 1/4 cup brown sugar
- 3 tbsp pure maple syrup
- 1/2 tsp maple flavoring
- 2 tbsp softened butter
- 1 1/2 cups powdered sugar
- 1/4 tsp vanilla
- 1/4 tsp maple flavoring
- 1 tsp salt
- 1 package yeast
- 1/4 cup warm water
- 1 egg, slightly beaten
- 4-5 cups flour

Directions

1. In a large microwave-safe bowl, heat the milk, butter, sugar and salt until the butter is just about all melted.
2. Stir to melt the rest of the butter.
3. Cool slightly. In a mixing bowl, combine the warm water and yeast until bubbly.
4. Add the egg to the milk mixture and then add to the yeast.

5. Either with a dough hook attachment on a heavy-duty mixer or with brute strength of your arm and spoon, add the flour and knead 5-10 minutes.
6. Cover in a bowl and let rise one hour until doubled.

Directions For Maple Pecan Breakfast Ring:

Punch down and roll out to a large rectangle (20 inches long).

Spread softened butter all over to edges.

Combine remaining filling ingredients and sprinkle evenly all over.

Roll up, jelly roll style.

Cut roll in half lengthwise and turn the cut sides up, next to each other.

Prepare large round pan and grease the outside of a ramekin, too.

Place the ramekin in the center of the round pan.

Twist the two halves of the cut dough and gently pick it up and place it in the prepared pan to form a ring. Pinch the ends together.

Cover and let rise 30 minutes.

Bake in a 375° preheated oven for 35-40 minutes or until golden brown.

Remove from oven and let cool in pan.

Make glaze by stirring softened butter into powdered sugar.

Combine the flavorings and a little water and add to the sugar/butter mixture.

Stir until smooth.

Add more water if necessary until you get the consistency you like.

Pour glaze over the top.

Serve warm or at room temperature.

If you enjoyed reading this book as much as I enjoyed writing it then be sure to return to the Amazon page and leave a review.

Go to Tonyakappes.com for a full reading order of my novels and while there join my newsletter. You can also find links to Facebook, Instagram and Goodreads.

Join like-minded readers like YOU in the Cozy Krew Facebook Group for dream casting, fan theories, and live Q & A's. It's like a BIG GIANT BOOK CLUB! But if you want to have your own book club, be sure you let me know! I love to send goodies.

Also By Tonya Kappes

A Camper and Criminals Cozy Mystery
BEACHES, BUNGALOWS, & BURGLARIES
DESERTS, DRIVERS, & DERELICTS
FORESTS, FISHING, & FORGERY
CHRISTMAS, CRIMINALS, & CAMPERS
MOTORHOMES, MAPS, & MURDER
CANYONS, CARAVANS, & CADAVERS
HITCHES, HIDEOUTS, & HOMICIDE
ASSAILANTS, ASPHALT, & ALIBIS
VALLEYS, VEHICLES & VICTIMS
SUNSETS, SABBATICAL, & SCANDAL
TENTS, TRAILS, & TURMOIL
KICKBACKS, KAYAKS, & KIDNAPPING
GEAR, GRILLS, & GUNS
EGGNOG, EXTORTION, & EVERGREENS
ROPES, RIDDLES, & ROBBERIES
PADDLERS, PROMISES, & POISON
INSECTS, IVY, & INVESTIGATIONS
OUTDOORS, OARS, & OATHS
WILDLIFE, WARRANTS, & WEAPONS
BLOSSOMS, BARBEQUE, & BLACKMAIL
LANTERNS, LAKES, & LARCENY
JACKETS, JACK-O-LANTERN, & JUSTICE
SANTA, SUNRISES, & SUSPICIONS
VISTAS, VICES, & VALENTINES
ADVENTURE, ABDUCTION, & ARREST
RANGERS, RV'S, & REVENGE
CAMPFIRES, COURAGE, & CONVICTS
TRAPPING, TURKEYS, & THANKSGIVING
GIFTS, GLAMPING, & GLOCKS

Kenni Lowry Mystery Series
FIXIN' TO DIE
SOUTHERN FRIED
AX TO GRIND
SIX FEET UNDER
DEAD AS A DOORNAIL
TANGLED UP IN TINSEL
DIGGIN' UP DIRT
BLOWIN' UP A MURDER

Killer Coffee Mystery Series
SCENE OF THE GRIND
MOCHA AND MURDER
FRESHLY GROUND MURDER
COLD BLOODED BREW
DECAFFEINATED SCANDAL
A KILLER LATTE
HOLIDAY ROAST MORTEM
DEAD TO THE LAST DROP
A CHARMING BLEND NOVELLA (CROSSOVER WITH MAGICAL
CURES MYSTERY)
FROTHY FOUL PLAY
SPOONFUL OF MURDER
BARISTA BUMP-OFF

Holiday Cozy Mystery
FOUR LEAF FELONY
MOTHER'S DAY MURDER
A HALLOWEEN HOMICIDE
CHOCOLATE BUNNY BETRAYAL
APRIL FOOL'S ALIBI
FATHER'S DAY MURDER
THANKSGIVING TREACHERY

SANTA CLAUSE SURPRISE
NEW YEAR NUISANCE

Mail Carrier Cozy Mystery
STAMPED OUT
ADDRESS FOR MURDER
ALL SHE WROTE
RETURN TO SENDER
FIRST CLASS KILLER
POST MORTEM
DEADLY DELIVERY
RED LETTER SLAY

Magical Cures Mystery Series
A CHARMING CRIME
A CHARMING CURE
A CHARMING POTION (novella)
A CHARMING WISH
A CHARMING SPELL
A CHARMING MAGIC
A CHARMING SECRET
A CHARMING CHRISTMAS (novella)
A CHARMING FATALITY
A CHARMING DEATH (novella)
A CHARMING GHOST
A CHARMING HEX
A CHARMING VOODOO
A CHARMING CORPSE
A CHARMING MISFORTUNE
A CHARMING BLEND (CROSSOVER WITH A KILLER COFFEE
COZY)
A CHARMING DECEPTION

A Southern Magical Bakery Cozy Mystery Serial
A SOUTHERN MAGICAL BAKERY

A Ghostly Southern Mystery Series
A GHOSTLY UNDERTAKING
A GHOSTLY GRAVE
A GHOSTLY DEMISE
A GHOSTLY MURDER
A GHOSTLY REUNION
A GHOSTLY MORTALITY
A GHOSTLY SECRET
A GHOSTLY SUSPECT

A Southern Cake Baker Series
(WRITTEN UNDER MAYEE BELL)
CAKE AND PUNISHMENT
BATTER OFF DEAD

Spies and Spells Mystery Series
SPIES AND SPELLS
BETTING OFF DEAD
GET WITCH or DIE TRYING

A Laurel London Mystery Series
CHECKERED CRIME
CHECKERED PAST
CHECKERED THIEF

A Divorced Diva Beading Mystery Series
A BEAD OF DOUBT SHORT STORY
STRUNG OUT TO DIE
CRIMPED TO DEATH

About Tonya

Tonya has written over 100 novels, all of which have graced numerous bestseller lists, including the USA Today. Best known for stories charged with emotion and humor and filled with flawed characters, her novels have garnered reader praise and glowing critical reviews. She lives with her husband and a very spoiled rescue cat named Ro. Tonya grew up in the small southern Kentucky town of Nicholasville. Now that her four boys are grown men, Tonya writes full-time in her camper she calls her SHAMPER (she-camper).

Learn more about her be sure to check out her website tonyakappes.com. Find her on Facebook, Twitter, BookBub, and Instagram

Sign up to receive her newsletter, where you'll get free books, exclusive bonus content, and news of her releases and sales.

If you liked this book, please take a few minutes to leave a review now! Authors (Tonya included) really appreciate this, and it helps draw more readers to books they might like. Thanks!

Cover artist: Mariah Sinclair: The Cover Vault

Made in the USA
Monee, IL
16 November 2022